MW00463489

A Girl in Mind

A Girl in Mind

Mark P. Dunn

Five Star • Waterville, Maine

First Edition
First Printing: May 2006

Published in 2006 in conjunction with Tekno Books
and Ed Gorman.

Set in 11 pt. Plantin by Christina S. Huff.

Printed in the United States on permanent paper.

Library of Congress Cataloging-in-Publication Data

Dunn, Mark P.
    A girl in mind / by Mark P. Dunn.—1st ed.
        p. cm.
      ISBN 1-59414-414-1 (hc : alk. paper)
      1. Young women—Fiction. 2. Grandfathers—Fiction.
    3. Maine—Fiction. 4. California—Fiction. 5. Psychopaths—
Fiction. 6. Psychological fiction. I. Title.
    PS3604.U5625G57 2006
    813'.6—dc22   2005034659

For my mother and father

Chapter 1

Blowing smoke out through his nose, Teddy Pearson dropped the cigarette butt to the ground and crushed it under the heel of his scuffed black uniform shoe. He was standing outside the main entrance of the Davies Clinic, and through a gap in the line of stunted pine trees ahead, he could just make out the distant lights of Stone Beach. Pinpricks of light in the dark.

Between him and the lights, the bay churned. It was an angry sea tonight; Teddy could hear the waves smashing on the beach down by the dock. There was supposed to be a snowstorm moving in overnight, and Teddy was hoping it would hold off long enough so that the ferry to and from the mainland wouldn't cancel its morning run. That would leave him alone on the island with Cora until the ferry got running, and Teddy figured he had just about enough stress in his life without prolonging his shift a moment longer than necessary.

With a thin hand that was white from cold, he reached into his Army fatigue jacket and pulled a pack of Camel Lights from an inside pocket, then lit another. It was his fifth in the past half-hour, and though Teddy wasn't usually a big smoker, he couldn't seem to stop himself. Last one, he thought, dragging hard, then rounds. He didn't want to miss the timer, after all. If it were allowed to buzz for more than two minutes without being reset, it would show up on his record for the night. He dragged deeply again, then closed his eyes and leaned back against the wall, pulling the coat more tightly about his narrow torso.

Teddy was exhausted, and for good reason. He'd spent the past three afternoons curled up on a child-sized cot in a room at the Eastern Maine Medical Center in Bangor, listening to the sound of his grandmother breathing, breathing, breathing, a husky, rattling noise rendered metronomic by the artificial respirator she was hooked up to. Over the weekend, she had suffered a major stroke. The only thing keeping her "alive" was the life-support, but the respirator could do nothing for her mind, which the doctors said was almost certainly damaged beyond hope of rehabilitation. But as dead as her brain might be, the respirator kept her going, hour after hour.

It was impossible to sleep listening to that sound, Teddy had found, impossible. And it was impossible not to listen to it. Lying in the cot he'd been provided with, which was about a foot too short, Teddy kept waiting for his grandmother's breathing to stop, signaling him that the end had come. But it didn't. Countless times he'd prayed for God to stop it, to stop the respirator from pumping air into her lungs. But in the end it wasn't God who made that decision.

At just after three this afternoon, Teddy had instructed the doctor in charge of his grandmother's care at Eastern Maine Medical Center to take her off the respirator. All the information the doctors had gathered said the same thing. She was never going to wake up. Never. He'd watched as her chest fell for the last time, some part of him still expecting it to rise again, proving that some part of her ravaged brain was still functioning. The woman who had raised Teddy from the age of six, when both his parents had died in a car wreck, was dead. With his grandmother gone, Teddy was alone. And so tired.

In the last week, spending his nights on the island at the Davies Clinic, to which he had been assigned a couple of weeks ago by MedPro, the temp service that passed on his nursing work, and his days at EMMC in Bangor, Teddy figured he'd slept no more than three or four hours a day. And it had taken its toll. He felt sick to his stomach perpetually; he'd been drinking as many as twenty cups of coffee a day, and the caffeine and sugar were burning viciously at his stomach lining. That he was smoking so much didn't help either. His throat was raw and his lungs had a burnt feel.

When he woke up to go to work, it hurt to open his eyes, and having them open never stopped causing him discomfort. It felt like grains of sand had been crammed beneath his eyelids and were scratching at his corneas like diamonds on glass. On top of all that, he hadn't had time to shower in days, and his skin was oily and dirty. His face ached from a dozen spots where pimples were pushing up, and his shoulder-length black hair, his best feature according to his just-departed grandmother, was heavy and greasy.

All Teddy wanted was to go home to his apartment and fall asleep, with no sound other than some Enya or Pink Floyd on low. All he wanted was to take a shower and sleep for days, to crawl beneath the quilt on his bed at home and do his best impersonation of one of the Clinic's patients. But despite his exhaustion, Teddy didn't feel like he'd ever be able to sleep again. Not until he came to some kind of peace about what he'd done. He prayed that some day he would be able to.

Teddy crushed out his cigarette and headed back inside, wincing at the drastic temperature change as he passed through the door.

He reached the duty-office just in time to watch the timer tick down to zeros: 00:0300:0200:01. He slapped the red

9

reset button on top of the timer before it could go off. The buzzing sound it emitted was loud and abrasive, and Teddy's nerves were shot already. No help needed in that department, thank you very much.

The clock reset to 60:00 and began counting down again.

With a resigned sigh, Teddy shrugged off his jacket and hung it over the back of a chair. It was time to do his job.

And his job was simple, really, simple as pie, now that the Clinic only had one patient left.

Every hour, Teddy made the rounds. The informal part of that duty involved checking that all the windows were secure, doors locked, that sort of thing. To ensure that the night shift RN made a full hourly circuit of the Clinic, Davies had installed a system of timers, one in each room. Once an hour, as in the duty office, the timers had to be reset.

The more official aspect of Teddy's duty was to make sure that the Clinic's patients were properly medicated, which was practically a non-issue since Cora Gardener was the only patient left. Earlier in the week, just a day or two after Cora was flown in from California, Doctor Davies had emptied the Clinic of all other patients, two young children and an older man. To Teddy it seemed obvious that the old doctor was clearing the Clinic of all his other patients so he could focus on Cora, and Teddy was fine with that. Dealing with one vegetable was a lot easier than dealing with four or five.

Teddy opened the office door and let himself out into the darkened hallway, then began his walk of the Clinic's perimeter.

The old Navy building which housed the Clinic was shaped like a T, with the duty office and storage rooms located in the shorter, transverse section of the building. The long arm housed the patient rooms, a couple of closets, and doctors' offices. During the Clinic's more prosperous days, Teddy guessed, there had been several doctors on staff, but now there were just two: Doctor Davies, the founder and owner of the Clinic, and Doctor Johnstone. He'd heard that when the Clinic's patients had been more numerous, Davies had employed two night shift RNs instead of just one, and a security guard to boot. Teddy thought it would have been nice to have some company out here. Spending the night alone six days a week was a drag. And creepy. There was no getting past that aspect of the job. Evidently, his predecessor hadn't been able to.

Part of the reason working the night shift at the Clinic was so creepy was that Teddy was allowed to turn on the lights only during his hourly rounds. Lighting the entire place cost a fortune, and since the moment he'd first arrived at the Clinic, Teddy had been acutely aware that the place was in some pretty severe financial straits.

And the monetary corner-cutting didn't end with the lights, either. Though each room in the Clinic was outfitted with a pair of security cameras, the system was completely shut down, and apparently had been for some time. The monitors in the duty office that Teddy presumed were hooked up to the cameras were covered in a thick layer of dust, and their tops were piled high with files and loose papers.

But the biggest reason working the night shift at the Davies Clinic gave Teddy the heebie jeebies was the old submarine base down below. On Teddy's first day, Davies had taken him aside and filled him in on what he needed to know, which, apparently, wasn't a whole hell of a lot. Just enough to get the old imagination cranking, but not enough to lend him any peace of mind.

During World War II, the building which housed the

Clinic had been a submarine base. Below the basement of the building, which housed the furnace room and some storage areas, there were several floors of deserted passageways. They were supposed to have been cleared out by the Navy long ago, but Davies had said, enough rumors of scavengable goods lingered that robbery remained a peripheral concern at the Clinic.

Teddy stopped in front of a door and unhooked the heavy metal ring of keys from his belt, flipped through them, then stuck one into the lock and turned it. The lock disengaged with a solid click and Teddy opened the door.

The room beyond was dark. Teddy slipped the big Mag Lite from its loop on his belt and switched it on, then panned it around the small room. The beam passed over a refrigerator, a table, and a couple of chairs. This was the staff kitchenette. During the day the door was propped open with a wooden door wedge, but it was closed and locked up at night because, well, everything was closed and locked up at night. All the doors in the Clinic were left over from the building's original use as a submarine base, and they all locked automatically when closed.

Teddy stepped to the counter on the far side of the room and hit the reset button on the timer, watching to make sure the red numbers reset to sixty minutes. Satisfied, he left the room and closed the door.

Moving quickly, Teddy repeated the process with the rest of the rooms on the short arm of the Clinic, then headed for the patient wing and started on the rooms there.

It didn't take him long to work his way through the fifteen vacant rooms in the hall. The beds were made and everything was in order. In the closet of one of the rooms, however, he did find a Winnie the Pooh backpack with a picture of Eeyore on the front. Stuffed inside were a worn blanket and some rumpled clothes. This had been Claudia's room, Teddy remembered. When she'd been moved out to Portland a couple of days ago, the bag must somehow have been left behind. Not a big surprise, though, he thought. Though he'd only been around for a short while, it was obvious that all was not well at the Davies Clinic. Teddy swung the bag over one of his shoulders and moved on with his rounds.

In about five minutes he was standing in front of Cora's door. He slipped the appropriate key into the lock and let himself in.

Cora was sleeping, but then, that's why she was at the Clinic, which specialized in the treatment and study of catatonia.

The sixteen-year-old lay on her back, hands at her sides. Her long brown hair was splayed out on her pillow and over her shoulders. It framed a face shaped by soft lines: a graceful nose, freckled at the top, full lips, high cheekbones, and thin crescent eyebrows. Her chest rose and fell in normal sleep rhythms. The EKG and EEG beeped softly in the background, the beep of the EKG high and sharp, the EEG pitched lower and slower.

Though normally Teddy would hardly have noticed the sounds, their effect on him now was profound, gut-wrenching. Only a few short hours ago, he'd stood in a room not so unlike this one, and given the order to let his grandmother die.

Doing his best to put those thoughts from his mind, Teddy set the backpack down by the door, walked to the counter running along one side of the room, and opened a drawer. He pulled out a syringe and drew twenty ccs of Paxidol from the vial on the counter, then plunged the needle into the girl's IV drip and pushed the stopper down. He recapped the syringe and dropped it into the white and blue hazardous waste disposal can near the door, also hitting the reset button on the room's timer, which sat on a metal tray beside Cora's bed.

After taking a quick look around the room to make sure everything else was in order, he picked Claudia's bag up and left, easing the door closed behind him.

Back in the office, Teddy tossed the bag into a corner and sat down in a swivel chair at the paper-littered desk. He felt strangely wired, stoked. The last thing he wanted to do right now was sit still. What he really wanted was another cigarette to settle his nerves. On the other hand, he knew that in about ten minutes he'd probably be fighting to stay awake. Better to save his cigarettes for when he really needed them.

He checked his watch: 2:19 a.m. Almost six more hours to go.

"Fuck," he sighed, surprising himself with the raw emotion in his voice. There were tears in his gritty eyes, and he wiped them away tiredly. It wasn't the first time he'd teared up tonight, and he figured it wouldn't be the last. He took a sip of lukewarm coffee from his mug on the desk, then leaned back and started waiting for three, when the buzzer on the desk would go off once more, reminding him that it was time to make the rounds again. Never a dull moment at the Davies Clinic, no siree, Bob.

At around 2:30 it began to snow, big flakes dropping fast. This was very bad news for Teddy, since if the snow got too heavy, the ferry wouldn't risk coming out to the island with the morning crew. Being stuck out here all day after a night shift was the last thing Teddy wanted. It would mean he'd have to keep on making hourly rounds until the ferry got running again, and God only knew how long that would take. People in Maine always said that if you don't like the weather just wait a minute, and that was often true, but the only thing that ever seemed to change was that it got worse and fucking worse with every second that passed.

Teddy stood and walked to the window, leaned his forehead against the glass to minimize the glare from the fluorescent lighting in the office, and stared out toward the mainland. He couldn't see the lights anymore, and the snow was coming down harder and faster every second, big flakes the size of bottle caps. In the wide ovals of light thrown by the floods mounted outside the office window, Teddy could see that the ground was already covered with the stuff.

The lamp of the island's lighthouse swung its strong beam out over the bay and toward Stone Beach, but all Teddy could see was a frenzy of blowing white. The Clinic may as well have been swallowed by a cloud.

Feeling hopeless, Teddy returned to the duty desk and sat back down.

Someone had left a mostly-finished crossword puzzle on the desk. Teddy picked it up and was reaching for a pen, when his eyes passed over what was written in the puzzle's spaces.

In large blue letters, just like the ones his grandmother had always used to fill out the crossword in the weekend edition of the *Bangor Daily News*, the words "HELP ME" had been written into every possible space. Where the proper number of spaces weren't available, the two-word phrase alternately overflowed the puzzle's boundaries or had been crammed into the space available.

With a gasp, Teddy dropped the folded newspaper to the floor and scooted away from it, sliding the wheeled swivel chair back so hard that he plowed into the wall behind the desk, banging his elbow hard.

"What the fuck?" he said, conscious that he was shaking, clutching the elbow he had hit against the wall with his other hand. He'd hit the funny bone, and shocks were still running up and down the arm, tingling his fingers.

As if sneaking up on a coiled snake, Teddy eased forward again, searching the floor for the crossword.

The folded newspaper had fallen beneath the desk. Only a wrinkled, gray corner was visible. Using the toe of his black shoe, Teddy pulled it the rest of the way out.

The big blue letters were gone. The puzzle looked as it had before: black ink, sloppy lowercase scrawl, a little more than half of the spaces filled in.

Letting out the breath he'd been holding, Teddy leaned over and picked up the puzzle, then pulled the chair back to the desk and sat down. He put the puzzle aside, however. Its allure had been lost.

Teddy pulled open the center drawer of the desk and rummaged inside. Beneath a smear of rumpled papers, he found a deck of cards. Thinking that a few games of Solitaire might help ease his nerves, Teddy started counting the cards.

He was at thirty-two when there was suddenly a loud sound from inside the office.

Teddy burst out of the chair and to his feet, arms raised protectively. His flailing hands sent the cards sailing in the direction of the door. It was only a second later that he realized the sound was the hourly buzzer going off.

Lowering his arms slowly, Teddy felt himself blushing. Even though there was nobody else around to see what he'd done, he was embarrassed. "Jesus, Theodore," he muttered sheepishly to himself, "get a pair, why dontcha?"

He slapped the timer's red button, cutting the buzzing sound off. The timer reset to sixty minutes.

Pulling the Mag Lite from his belt, Teddy headed for the door of the office. He was halfway there when it dawned on him why the timer had startled him so much. It had come too

16

soon. Way too soon. He looked up at the clock above the door and what it said confirmed his suspicion. It was only 2:35. The buzzer shouldn't have gone off for almost another half-hour.

That's strange, Teddy thought. He'd never noticed a problem with the system before. He'd have to write it up in the log so Davies could have it fixed. Shoving the flashlight back into its loop, Teddy turned back toward the desk to record the timer error in the duty-log, but something on the floor caught his attention instead.

The cards he'd dropped should have been scattered all over the floor, but they weren't. They'd been arranged into a rough pattern, though a recognizable one.

Laid out flat on the floor, end to end, the red Bicycle playing cards formed one word: HELP.

Blood rushed to Teddy's head and he felt faint. "No," he said, closing his eyes. "Please." He pressed his eyes shut as tightly as he could. When he opened them, the word was gone. The cards were scattered all over the floor.

He moved to pick them up, then changed his mind and grabbed a broom and a dustpan from the utility closet just outside the office. He quickly swept the cards into the pan, then emptied it into the garbage can. It made him feel a little bit better, but he thought he knew something that would help out more.

Time for a cigarette break, he thought, taking his jacket from the back of the swivel chair and pulling it on. Time for a long motherfucking cigarette break. He left the office and headed for the front entrance, keenly anticipating the first drag. *Shit,* he thought as he reached the intersection of the long and short hallways, *I do believe I'm becoming an addict.*

"Teddy."

He stopped in his tracks, almost literally frozen. Every muscle in his body was strained to the snapping point.

That was his grandmother's voice, and it had sounded so close. Where had it come from? Inside him? His mind? Had he said it himself? It was entirely possible that he had, he supposed. As tired as he was, he wouldn't have been surprised at anything he did. Still, it had sounded so much like her.

Teddy let out a quavering breath. He was shaking again, hard. A cigarette. He really needed a cigarette.

He started again toward the front entrance of the Clinic, but he hadn't gotten two steps before he heard the voice again, clearer this time.

"Teddy, help me. Please . . ." It was coming from somewhere at the end of the long hallway.

Teddy stopped and clamped his hands over his ears, pressing his eyes closed once again. "Stop it!" he yelled. "Shut the fuck up!" All he wanted was to be outside, away from this place.

But Christ if he wasn't turning down the long hallway.

Why? he thought. *Why am I going down there? It's not my grandmother saying those things; my grandmother is dead. I killed her myself, just this afternoon.*

No, another voice came in, reproachful, *you let her die peacefully, the way she would have wanted.*

But I'll never know. Never know . . . What if she didn't want to die yet? What if she hates me for what I did?

Cora's room was coming up on the left.

Teddy took the keys from his belt and fitted the right one into the lock, surprised at how calm he suddenly felt. He twisted the key in the lock, then pushed the door open.

There she was. His grandmother, pale, still, her gray-purple hair puffed out on the pillow like a storm cloud, her eyes deep in their sockets, shadowy.

"But where's Co—"

His grandmother's eyes flicked open and her head turned

18

toward him. In their dark holes, her eyes were bright, alert, desperate.

"*Help me,*" she said, "*I'm still here. Don't give up.*"

Teddy felt something give away inside his head, a nearly physical rupture. He slammed the door to Cora's room and started running as fast as he could.

The next thing he knew, he had a lit cigarette in his mouth and was using the blade of his Swiss Army knife to saw through the rope securing the Clinic's Boston Whaler to its cleat in the boathouse.

The bay doors of the boathouse were open, and the scene beyond was a choppy vista of swirling snow and breaking whitecap waves. He finished cutting the last few strands of rope, wondering even as he did why he hadn't just untied the rope from the cleat, then climbed into the rocking boat and yanked the rip-cord of the outboard engine. The motor was cold, and it took a couple of tries to get it started, but it finally did, spitting a cloud of oily black smoke.

Teddy twisted the throttle and the boat moved ahead into the bay. He could hear himself talking, but he couldn't tell what he was saying. He thought he might just have been laughing.

A little after 5:45 the next morning, a Stone Beach woman named Emily Garfield chased her feisty black lab puppy down Main Street toward the docks. It was still dark and would be for another hour at least, but Emily had to be all the way over in Ellsworth by 7:30 for an appointment with her OB-GYN, and now, when she was already running late, Jesse, the pup, had caught her at a distracted moment and torn the leash from her hands.

Little bastard, she thought, then immediately felt guilty and resolved to give Jesse an extra scoop of food when she got him back home. She could never stay mad for long; it just wasn't in her makeup.

Halfway down the hill, she stopped, sliding and nearly falling on the poorly shoveled sidewalk.

A man was walking toward her from the direction of the docks. In his hand he held Jesse's leash, and the pup padded along beside him, surprisingly docile. As the man approached, Emily realized that he was wearing only a pair of what looked like hospital scrubs, and that he was soaking wet and shaking violently from the cold. With one of his shaking hands, he held the leash out and Emily took it. As she did, her hand brushed his and she felt how very cold he was. He shouldn't even be walking around, Emily thought. He should be lying somewhere unconscious.

"Thank you," she said, but the pale, shaking young man never even stopped; he just continued up the hill, the way Emily had just come, weaving a little from side to side.

Emily watched him until he reached the top of the hill and turned left on Sudbury Street, then remembered her appointment and, towing Jesse along behind her, set off for home.

Chapter 2

Cole Johnstone took one last sip of coffee from the blue and white Duke University coffee mug, then set it down on the small table just inside the door of his apartment. The cream-colored liquid inside the mug was too sweet and too milky, but the pot had been sitting on the burner since he'd woken up at 6:30, and there were only so many ways to mask the foul taste of burnt coffee, and cheap burnt coffee at that. Anyway, after nights like his, Cole needed all the sugar and caffeine he could get.

Grimacing with anticipation of the cold he knew would greet him outside, he took his black Gore-Tex coat from its hook beside the door and shrugged it on, zipping it tightly up around his neck.

He made sure he had his keys and gloves, then left his second-floor apartment, pulling the door shut behind him, jiggling the knob to ensure that the lock had engaged.

Outside on his porch, it was no warmer and no colder than he'd expected. The overhang partially concealed a slate gray sky that looked as darkly ominous as it had for the past month, this despite the foot and a half of snow they'd gotten last night and into the morning. Almost 11:00 now, it was hardly brighter out than it had been when he'd been woken by a phone call. Opening his eyes, the first thing he'd seen had been the view out his bedroom window. He'd known whom the call was from before he'd even said hello. It was the Stone Beach Ferry's office. No morning run; he'd have to wait till noon.

Holding tightly to the railing that some expeditious soul had already wiped clear of snow, Cole made his way cautiously down the wooden stairs to the ground level. Once there, he stomped across the white lawn separating his building from the street, stepping in ragged footprints likely made by the same kind pilgrim who'd done such a wonderful job on the staircase.

Main Street had been plowed, but then he'd known it would be. That was the thing about Maine. It snowed and snowed, but things never ground to a halt the way they did in other places. A plow just came along, and life kept on keeping on. The sidewalks had also been blown clear of snow, and Cole was able to make his way fairly quickly down the few blocks to the Stone Beach marina, where he crossed the street at the town's only traffic light and hurried down to the marina's main jetty.

Most of the slips were empty; the fishing and lobster boats didn't cater to the weather. Fair or foul, they went about their work, day in and day out.

The ferry bobbed gently at the end of the long dock and, as Cole approached, he could see Manny, the ferry's captain, standing in the transom, speaking animatedly to one of his mates, a young boy of seventeen or eighteen. Manny was no taller than five-three or -four, but was wide chested and looked strong: an imposing, if vertically diminutive, figure.

As Cole stepped over the edge of the hull and onto the ship, Manny noticed him and smiled.

"Hello, Doctor Johnstone," he said, turning his attention briefly away from the boy. "Beautiful morning, eh?"

Manny was a full-blooded Italian, dark-skinned and black-haired, and Cole thought he seemed sorely out of place amidst all the snow. He thought the ferry's short captain would look a thousand times more at ease on the rocky shores of the Mediterranean.

"Kid giving you trouble?" Cole said.

Manny threw up his hands, palms to the sky, an expression of pure exasperation on his face. "Two times this week, the boy has forgotten to throw off the aft lines. Two times! Only pure luck we didn't rip the dock down."

"Give him a break, Manny. He's just young." Cole saw the boy give him a thankful glance, but it was short-lived.

Manny slashed both hands through the air violently and said, "No break!" Just before he turned his full attention back to the boy, Manny slipped Cole a sly wink and a grin.

Making his way to the back of the boat, Cole heard the Italian's voice rising. He had a feeling the boy wouldn't forget to toss the aft lines again.

Cole took his customary seat just outside the rear entrance to the cabin. There were seats inside, and it would be much warmer in there, but for Cole the only thing worse than being on a boat was being inside on a boat. That only intensified his already powerful feeling of claustrophobia.

Buckling down for the ride, he crossed his arms over his chest and dug his gloved hands underneath his armpits, trying to conserve body heat.

Five minutes or so later, when the last of the ferry's passengers had boarded, the boat pulled out of its slip and headed out into the bay.

As the engine picked up its pace, Cole glanced into the cabin through the partially clouded windows and saw Doctor Davies seated in a corner, sipping coffee from a brown paper cup. The Clinic's day shift RN sat inside the cabin also, a substantially overweight girl from town named Dana. She was sitting as far from Davies as she could, while still remaining in the cabin. Cole couldn't suppress a grim chuckle.

This is perfect, he thought, *absolutely perfect. We are as dysfunctional as any family I've ever seen, and we're supposed to be in the business of helping people.*

The island that housed the Davies Clinic was the ferry's first stop. From there Manny would pilot the boat through the maze of small fishing islands and rich residential islands that peppered the bay, then return to port in Stone Beach, only to repeat the process a few hours later. As Cole stepped off the boat and onto the island's sole dock, it occurred to him that no matter how miserable his job could be at times, it would never be as routine and redundant as Manny's.

Not bothering to wait for Davies and Dana, Cole started up the long path that led to the Clinic's front door, forcing his way through the knee-high snow.

As he passed the boathouse, he heard a banging sound and stopped. Looking to his right, he noticed that the door was unlatched, opening and closing in the wind, slapping the jamb. There were dimples in the deep snow leading from the main path toward the boathouse, as if someone had been out here last night, before the bulk of the snow had fallen.

He left the path and moved toward the small building. Reaching it, he pushed the door all the way open and looked inside.

It was too dark to see anything. He groped along the wall for the light switch, found it, and flicked it up.

The overhead lights buzzed and flickered into life.

The boathouse's one large room was empty. Not just of people, but completely empty. The Whaler was gone.

Cole walked to the front of the boat slip and stooped to pick up the rope that usually moored the Whaler to its cleat. About two feet from the cleat, the rope had been cut cleanly.

It hadn't frayed or rotted; the cut was on a pronounced diagonal and there weren't any ragged edges. It was as though the rope had been severed by a scalpel or something equally sharp.

Dropping the rope, Cole stood with a perplexed grunt and left the boathouse, continuing on his way to the Clinic. *Davies is just going to love this,* he thought, *absolutely love it.*

He let himself in the front door and stopped at his office to shuck off his coat before heading down to Davies' office to tell him about the missing boat.

There was already a yellow slip atop the pile of files and loose papers on his desk, a note saying that he was expected to meet with Davies in around half an hour, at 12:30. The note was in Dana's childlike handwriting. Cole shook his head wearily at Davies. Even with the precipitous decline in the prosperity of his Clinic, the old man wouldn't, or couldn't, lower himself enough in his own estimation to write his own goddamned notes. Unbelievable. In order for Dana to get him the note so quickly, Davies must have recited it to her on the way up from the ferry.

Suddenly bone-tired, Cole slumped down into his swivel chair, feeling deflated. He needed more coffee, but couldn't summon the energy it would take to rise and walk to the duty-office to make some.

It could wait, he decided. The Whaler could wait. Everything could wait.

Cole let his eyes close, leaned back in his chair, and rested his head against the wall, propping his feet up on the corner of his desk. His body felt as though it was weighed down with sandbags at the wrists, ankles, and midsection, as did his mind. He sank quickly out of consciousness and into the familiar benthic realm of his dreams, which started just as they had for the past six years. Only this time there was an added

darkness, an almost electrical ominousness, and Cole almost woke up before . . . it was no use; sleep claimed him.

He sat on the piano bench, alone in the living room of the old house in Quincy.

Afternoon sunlight slanted in past the drawn curtains, the cream-colored ones with the red and yellow and pink roses, the ones Jessica had sewn years ago.

Very green trees blew gently in the summer breeze outside the window, and a lone squirrel scavenged what it could from the house-shaped bird feeder in the front lawn.

In his hands, Cole held a gray, stuffed elephant.

Jimmy's elephant.

The tag was still attached to the animal's ear. Cole gripped the paper tightly and yanked, pulling the tag free, then dropping it on the glass table in front of him.

From outside, there was a commotion, a chorus of voices raised in unison. Cole grinned, envisioning Jimmy playing soccer or Frisbee with the rest of the kids. He stood to go watch, still holding the gray elephant, toting the small animal by its curled trunk.

The living room was decorated with blue and red and yellow streamers that twisted in from the four corners of the room, meeting in the middle. A multi-colored HAPPY BIRTHDAY banner spanned the doorway between the living room and the dining room. Cole ducked to pass beneath it.

Still listening to the sound of the voices from outside, voices that didn't sound quite right for some reason, Cole's eyes moved quickly over the dining room table, where one last piece of Jimmy's cake remained. The triangular slab of vanilla cake was iced with chocolate. Written sloppily in green across the top of the piece was JIMMY. Jessica always saved their son his name piece.

Beginning to feel the slightest bit of apprehension because the

voices hadn't died down, Cole opened the sliding glass door and stepped out onto the screened-in porch.

It was a bright day, and all Cole could see as he pushed the door of the porch open and exited onto the deck was that a throng of people had gathered in front of the pool.

As his eyes adjusted to the light, he realized that it wasn't merely a crowd of people, but that it was EVERYONE, all of the children and adults he and Jessica had invited to celebrate Jimmy's fifth birthday. And he realized that the summer day was now almost soundless. Almost. From somewhere in the center of all those people, a keening scream, breathless. And it sounded like Jessica.

Cole took two hesitant steps, then broke into a sprint. Though there must have been fifty feet between him and the pool; he covered the distance in seconds, plunging into the gathered people, pushing them out of his way, saying, "Move . . . get the fuck out of my way . . . move, move."

Breaking through into the center.

Jessica kneeling on the ground, wearing her red one-piece bathing suit, a towel wrapped around her waist, another coming undone from around her hair, slumping over her shoulders.

Resting on her lap, a child's head. White, wet body, red chest, blue swimming trunks. Jimmy's trunks.

Cole dropped to his knees beside his wife. Her hands were vise-tight over their son's face, blocking his features.

"Let go," Cole said, intending to give his son CPR. "Let go!" When she didn't, he drew back his hand and slapped her hard, meaning to catch her in the cheek, but hitting her instead in the side of the head, near the ear, throwing her off balance.

She let out another strangled scream and fell to the side, releasing the boy's face, but as Cole bent to press his mouth to Jimmy's, he saw that it wasn't Jimmy at all.

Cora lay motionless on the ground and, as Cole pulled back in confusion, her eyes snapped open and through a mouth that he could see was full of foul water, she said, "Help—"

Cole jolted awake and shot to his feet as if electrified.

"What the fuck was that?" he gasped. "What the fuck was that?"

He put his hands to his head and let out a retching sob, then leaned back against the wall and tried to gather himself.

When he could, he opened his eyes and saw the clock on the wall above the door: 12:35. He was late for his meeting with Davies.

"Shit," he muttered, wiping wetness from his cheek, trying to forget the dream. But, of course, he couldn't.

He left his office and headed down the hall at a jog, pulling on his waist-length white lab coat as he went.

Nearing Davies' door, Cole slowed to a walk, trying to regain his composure, straightening his white coat and blue tie as best he could, which wasn't very well since both the coat and tie had spent the night crumpled on the floor beside his bed. He ran his fingers once through his short, brown hair and then, ruefully, over his cheeks, which were covered with at least two days' worth of coarse stubble. Man, he thought, I must look like absolute shit. A state not improved by the sudden appearance of Cora in his dream, the same dream he'd been having, unaltered, for more than six years. Why the change? Why now?

On one hand, it seemed perfectly natural for him to be preoccupied with the girl. Her situation was heartbreaking, and no doubt he felt some empathy for the enormous loss she'd suffered. But he'd dealt with children before, dozens, even since Jimmy's death, and he'd never experienced anything remotely like this.

Though he once would have thought he'd welcome any

change in his dreams, no matter how small, he was no longer sure he felt that way. As terrifying and grueling as it was to re-experience the death of his only son each night and day, whenever he closed his eyes for the briefest of moments, now that it had been taken from him, he realized that the dream represented his last link to Jimmy. It seemed almost an affront that the dream should continue, but without his son.

He forced himself out of his reverie as he reached Davies' door and tried to focus on the situation at hand. What did Davies want?

Cole knocked twice assertively, a trick he'd adopted from his college roommate at Duke, who was perpetually late to everything. If you can't make it on time, his roommate had told him, don't pretend that you tried. Just act like you own the world, and that the world, therefore, runs according to your timepiece, not theirs.

"Come in," Davies called.

Bracing himself, Cole opened the door and entered Dr. Davies' office, shutting the door quietly behind him.

Davies was examining a file on his desk and didn't look up at Cole as he entered, so Cole sat down in one of the two over-stuffed, red chairs facing Davies' desk. They were the kind of high-backed, throne-like chairs that belonged in a Tudor mansion beside a roaring fireplace, not in a crowded little office on a remote island in Maine.

While Davies read, bald head bowed to the task, arms resting on the big walnut desk, Cole really looked at the old doctor for the first time in a long time, maybe since the day Davies had hired him two years ago.

He looked tired. Exhausted, really. It was no secret around the Clinic that Cora Gardner was his granddaughter and that Davies was taking her situation very much to heart. The change in his demeanor since her arrival was nothing short of drastic; he'd become more and more withdrawn over the past couple of weeks and, though he'd hardly been gregarious before, it was all Cole could do now to get a "hello" and "how are you?"

It wasn't so long ago that Harold Davies had been one of the most respected psychiatrists in the country, if not the world, a leader in the field of catatonia studies. And now, on top of all the myriad other troubles the Clinic was experiencing, the poor guy couldn't figure out how to help his own granddaughter.

Cole's heart went out to Davies and he wished, not for the first time, that the two of them were on good enough terms to talk about their troubles in detail. He thought there were things he could say to the man that could help.

Cora had come in just as the Clinic's two other patients were being transferred out to hospitals on the mainland, one in Portland, the other in San Diego.

It had quickly spread around the small remaining staff of the Clinic that the girl was there because her family—Davies' daughter Miranda, son-in-law Vince, and young grandson Alex—had been murdered in Los Angeles just days ago. It was something Davies never mentioned to anyone, including Cole.

Davies had initially taken Cora's case himself, and for more than a week had worked day and night running tests and researching possible treatments, but nothing had worked. His granddaughter was physically unharmed, but deeply comatose, and nothing Davies tried was able to change that.

Finally, sick and verging on complete collapse, he had asked Cole, who had been serving more or less as Davies' assistant and secretary in the absence of any other patients, to take over partial treatment of Cora.

That was just over a week ago. There had still been no

change in Cora's condition, and Cole had found himself becoming more and more invested in the case. He wanted to help this girl, and there was no denying any longer that he brought to this situation more than simply a professional interest. At the same time, though, he was becoming increasingly certain that his remaining time at the Clinic was limited, and that before long he'd be let go, as most of the Clinic's staff already had been.

Davies finished reading the file on his desk and looked up at Cole.

Underneath the older man's somnolent brown eyes, there were dark, purplish bags of wrinkly skin that his thick black-rimmed glasses magnified grotesquely. Cole didn't know how old Davies was, but at that moment he looked no younger than eighty.

"Take a look at this," Davies said, sliding the open file across the desk towards Cole. His voice was rough, wet, as though impeded on its path from his lungs. When he breathed, Cole heard a light rattle, and he wondered if the old man knew he was exhibiting symptoms of pneumonia, or if he was so deeply involved in the care of his granddaughter that all awareness of his own physical status had fled his obsessed mind.

Cole picked up the file and scanned the top page quickly. It was the timesheet of the new night shift RN from the temp agency, Teddy Pearson. The name wasn't familiar; Cole didn't think he'd ever met the man. That really wasn't too surprising, though, despite the small staff of the Clinic. If Pearson was a night shift RN, the only place he and Cole would cross paths would be on the Clinic's dock during shift exchange, and Cole tended to keep to himself during his daily trips to and from the island. He hated the water, though he was too stubborn to admit that he was terrified of it.

"What's this all about?" Cole asked, looking up from the file.

"It's about Mr. Pearson," Davies answered. "He went missing last night. Nobody knows where he is."

"Missing?" Cole said, surprised despite his earlier discovery. Then he quickly added, "Oh, wait, the Whaler's gone, too."

"How do you know that?"

Cole told him about seeing the boathouse door swinging open and closed in the wind, and the cut rope that usually moored the little motorboat in its slip.

As he spoke, Davies leaned back in his chair and steepled his fingers, listening intently. When Cole finished, Davies harrumphed and said, "Well, that makes no sense."

"What?" Cole got the impression that Davies wasn't referring just to the fact that an RN would steal a boat and desert his post.

Davies gestured with a hand at the file in front of Cole. "Notice anything odd about the timesheet?"

Cole looked back down at the yellow sheet the computer in the duty office printed off at the end of each shift and, after a brief examination, said, "There are no reset punches after two a.m." He raised his hand to his mouth and chewed thoughtfully on his ragged thumbnail, a bad habit he'd held onto since childhood. "That is strange, isn't it?" Why in the world would an RN abandon his post at 2:00 in the morning, especially when there was a blizzard blowing outside, making navigation by water all but impossible? For the first time Cole considered the chance that this wasn't a cut-and-dried case of dereliction of duty. Something entirely different could have happened. Robbery was the first thing that entered Cole's head. "Is anything missing?"

Davies shook his head. "I've already checked all the equipment and the medicine stocks. Everything's here. At least, everything I know to check for. There's always . . ." Davies tapped the floor with his foot so that Cole could hear.

He was referring to the abandoned submarine base underneath the Clinic, that had supposedly been stripped clean by the Navy long ago, but that still attracted enough rumors of scavengable goods to be of some minor worry.

The only entrance to the abandoned base, an elevator shaft that descended through the base's three levels, was located in the basement, beyond the boiler room. Access to the basement itself was restricted, however, by several locks on the door atop the staircase leading down from the Clinic, all of which could be unlocked from the inside with turn-bolts. This was a safety measure Davies had been forced to implement years ago. Also, the elevator car had long ago been dismantled and removed, leaving just the empty shaft.

The only people allowed now in the basement were workers from the company that serviced the old furnace periodically. Not even Davies retained a set of keys. Three years ago, a thirteen-year-old patient had somehow come into possession of a set and climbed down into the base. He'd only been found much later, and much too late. After his death, and the lawsuit that followed, the Clinic had been heavily fined and was even now just barely clinging to existence. The only thing keeping it alive was Davies' lingering reputation as a master with comatose children, and bringing them back.

"You think Pearson robbed the old base?"

"No," Davies said, "I don't. That just wouldn't make any sense. It would be idiotic."

He was right, Cole knew. For one thing, if Pearson was thinking about robbing the abandoned base, why would he do it on a night he was scheduled to work? That would automatically put him under suspicion, especially if he simply disappeared afterwards. It would make much more sense to come out alone during someone else's shift, when there was no evidence to place him at the scene.

"Are you going to call the police?" Cole asked, pretty sure he knew the answer before his query was even voiced.

With the Clinic teetering dangerously close to the steep precipice of nonexistence, Cole knew the last thing Davies wanted was to attract this sort of negative attention. It was a missing person that had nearly shut the Clinic down three years ago, and the report of another might just do the trick. Already, the number of patients entrusted to the Clinic by their families had dwindled, remaining just high enough to keep the place going; with the report of a missing staff person, who knew what could happen? If it had been a state-subsidized facility, the Clinic would no doubt have gone under three years ago, but owing to its status as a private clinic and to Davies' still-respected name, it continued to hang on by the skin of its teeth.

"No," Davies said, confirming Cole's hunch. "Not yet, anyway. What I think happened is that Mr. Pearson decided he didn't care much for this job and left in the boat early this morning, maybe with a few pills in his pocket, the sort of stuff we wouldn't miss right away unless we ran a thorough check, like Buspar or Prozac."

That explanation would make more sense than Cole knew Davies liked to admit. The Clinic was a pretty dismal place to work, two miles removed from the mainland as it was. Cole was sure that spending the night out on the island alone could be a real pisser, too. Spending five days a week on the island was bad enough.

It made sense for other reasons, too. Soon after Cole had arrived, the low number of patients at the Clinic had forced Davies to make cuts in the number of doctors and RNs on staff. In the old days, when fifteen or more rooms had consistently been filled, there were commonly two RNs and a security guard on night-detail alone, but within the past six months the Clinic's financial straits had become so serious that Davies had been forced to cut both the guard and one of the RNs. To make matters even worse, the quality of the RNs Davies could afford to hire had dropped precipitously, too. Most of them were temps who had turned permanent or had some sort of minor blemishes on their records: nothing outrageous, but significant enough to keep them from getting comparable jobs elsewhere. Cole himself knew all too well how that went. If it weren't for a six-month stay in an alcohol rehab clinic in Philadelphia five years ago, Cole wouldn't have been at the Clinic, either.

But still, he found it strange that Pearson would have just up and left in the middle of the night, especially the way it had been storming. It would have been practically suicidal.

There were other possibilities, but Cole shunted the one that immediately sprang to mind into the back of his skull, where it hummed like a bumblebee in a jar. More dangerous to let that bee out now that it had been trapped for a spell, getting pissed off; better just to keep it cooped up, or better yet, to fill the jar with water and drown the fucking thing. He threw the likeliest alternative out in front of Davies, instead.

"Or," Cole said, "he headed down to the dock this morning to catch the ferry, slipped on some ice, fell into the water, and hit his head, in which case we really should call the police."

"There's no way he could have assumed the ferry would run this morning," Davies countered. "It was practically a blizzard going on out there. We couldn't even get out here until noon."

Cole nodded. After a moment's hesitation, during which

he summoned and summarily dismissed any concern for the tenuous status of his own employment, Cole said, "Have you considered the possibility that Cora—"

"No," Davies snapped, spitting the word out before Cole could finish the thought. "And I think we're finished here. Good-bye, Cole." There was an angry flush in Davies' cheeks, lending a little color to the doctor's otherwise pallid face.

Feeling chastened and somewhat pissed at being brushed off so brusquely, Cole stood and left the office quickly, shutting the door a little too hard behind himself. He heard Davies break into a fit of moist-sounding coughing as he walked down the hall.

He seethed all the way back to his office and slumped angrily down into his uncomfortable swivel chair, all of his prior pity for Davies gone like smoke in the wind. He didn't know what he'd been thinking of, in trying to bring his suspicions about Cora up, but goddamn if Davies wasn't one stubborn son-of-a-bitch.

Cole tried to calm himself down. This kind of thinking wasn't productive in the least. Davies was just concerned for his granddaughter. That was all. Under the same circumstances, Cole was certain he would feel very much the same way: protective and standoffish, even to a fault.

But it just seemed like too much of a coincidence.

Just after Cora had arrived on the island, members of the Clinic's staff, including Cole, had started to see things that made no sense. Dana reported seeing an unfamiliar man walking around the Clinic and outside on the grounds, and Cole himself had seen, or had thought he'd seen, the faint image of an enormous blue bridge stretching off into the ocean. After he'd seen it though, just as he was climbing off the morning ferry, he'd been unable to say with any certainty that it hadn't just been a trick of the morning light. It had been there and gone in a single moment. The rest of the Clinic's staff seemed to feel the same way about what they'd seen, so nothing major was made of it.

Cole had made the mistake of talking to Davies about these sightings, and the old doctor had reacted violently, going so far as to threaten Cole with the loss of his position if he ever brought it up again. And so Cole hadn't. In the back of his mind, though, he had formed a certainty that Davies had seen things, too, and was simply unable to accept them as real. That was why he was being so obstinate, so stubborn. And while Cole couldn't blame the man, it was hard to know that he was right, or at least that he might be right, and still not be able to do anything.

Cole drummed his fingers on the arms of his chair and blew his breath out through his teeth.

A moment later he stood up and headed back down to Davies' office, mind made up.

He knocked on the door, but there was no answer.

"Doctor Davies?" he said. He knocked again, harder. "Doctor Davies?" He wondered where Davies could have gone. He hadn't left the old man's office more than two minutes ago.

When there was still no answer, Cole tried the knob. The door was still unlocked and swung open.

Davies was slumped over his desk, face to the side. His eyes were open and he appeared to be trying to sit up, though without much success.

"Don't move," Cole said, rushing to Davies' side. "Just stay still; it's going to be okay."

He picked up the phone on Davies' desk and punched the intercom button for the duty-office. Dana had apparently finished administering Cora her meds and answered right away.

"Dana," he said, "it's Doctor Johnstone. Get down to Doctor Davies' office immediately with a gurney, and call the Stone Beach police. We need the ferry out here pronto, and an ambulance to meet us at the dock on the mainland. Got that?"

"Got it," she said, reacting well, for which Cole was thankful, then clicked off.

A thirty-foot police launch arrived an hour later, a young cop from the Stone Beach PD at the helm. Cole made sure Davies was well wrapped in several of the Clinic's blankets, then helped the cop get the old doctor's stretcher aboard.

"Ambulance there?" Cole asked, nodding toward the distant shore as he climbed back off the boat.

The cop nodded and said, "There will be."

Cole watched until the launch was on its way with Davies, then went back inside to his office.

Sitting down behind his desk, Cole flipped to *D* in the ancient Rolodex he'd had for about a thousand years and grabbed the phone. This wasn't what Davies would have wanted, but goddamn if he was in a position to argue about it.

Cole dialed quickly, making a call he should have made a long time ago.

Chapter 3

Luis woke from the dream and lay still, breathing, breathing. He felt the texture of the cotton sheets underneath his naked body; he felt the sweat running in hot streams down the creases in his skin.

The dream was the same as it had been every night for the last two weeks. The black Mustang, his black Mustang, rocketing down a deserted highway toward the rising sun, passing signs for towns and cities, moving ever eastward, moving farther and farther away from Los Angeles. It was not a nightmare in the conventional sense, but Luis was scared, nonetheless. The usual headache pounded in his skull and he waited for it to pass, knowing that even when it did, he would still be able to feel it there, lurking.

Since Luis had been a child, one thing had remained constant about the dreams he remembered when he woke, and that was there were none. But now . . .

He sat up and swung his legs over the edge of the bed. The smell of sweat and sex in the room was strong. There was another smell, too, but Luis chose to disregard it for now.

He pulled on a pair of briefs and a T-shirt, then went to the kitchen and cracked some eggs for an omelet, still trying to shake the feeling of unease the dream had left him with.

The freezer was crammed full of frozen dinners and bags of gourmet coffee. Luis sorted through them, then chose a dark Arabian blend he'd come to like recently. After he'd started a pot brewing, he went to the bathroom, pissed, and sprinkled some lime lye over Kim, who was laid out on the floor atop a thick plastic tarp folded in two. He'd have to get her into a tub in the bedroom soon, before she started running all over the place. Already she didn't look so good.

The night's Polaroids were on the kitchen table where he'd tossed them before bed. Luis picked them up and examined them. Kim at the door to the bedroom, where he'd asked her to pose when they got back to his place from the bar, a sexy grin on her face. Kim minus her shirt and bra, the same grin still in place. Kim with a large kitchen knife handle-deep in her chest, not smiling anymore.

He opened the cabinet under the sink and reached under it, felt along the top of the cabinet for the flat leather pouch, found it, and pulled it out. He unzipped it and added Kim's pictures to his collection, making sure they were marked on the back with the appropriate numbers, then replaced the little brown satchel in its hiding place.

He ate and shaved and showered, then dressed in a sharply creased pair of khaki pants and a crisp blue button-down, finishing the outfit off with a nice Brooks Brothers tie he'd bought himself for Christmas the year before, and a pair of black dress shoes he'd seen in the window of Structure and coveted for weeks before finally giving in and buying them. Clothes taken care of, Luis clipped and filed his fingernails, then headed to work, feeling a little more human, feeling pretty good actually, except for the lingering pain in his head.

The night before had been rough. Picking kids up off the street wasn't what it used to be, even five years before. It was dangerous now. Half of them had switchblades, and the ones that didn't were almost always packing something else: a gun, a blackjack, something. Kim had a knife, wore it strapped to her thigh, but she'd been no trouble once he fed her a few whiskey sours laced with Valium. No trouble at all after that.

A pack of teenagers crossed the street in front of his Mustang. He revved the engine loudly and several of them jumped and sprinted to the other side of the road, peering back over their shoulders. One of the little fuckers, a boy with blue-dyed hair and the crotch of his baggy jeans hanging down to his knees, turned around and flipped him off. Luis couldn't help grinning, not at the little bastard's boldness, but at his mental picture of the way the cocksucker's guts would look strung up around his bedroom like Christmas lights.

The dream. Always his thoughts returned to the dream.

Black car, empty highway, movement, movement, and the direction always east, never shifting from that direction, through the desert, through the mountains, over the empty plains. Why east? What was there? Luis slammed his hands on the steering wheel. Even when he wasn't thinking about it, it was there, eating at him, occupying the back of his brain like a tumor, getting bigger and stronger every day and every night. His head throbbed with the remembrance of pain, the pain of those strange headaches.

The headaches terrified him. The thought that there might be a blood clot or a tumor growing inside his brain stalked him all day. It was terrifying, the fact that he might be dead already, but just wasn't sharp enough to have figured it out yet.

Luis turned left on La Brea and a few minutes later pulled into a space at the station.

"Hey, Argento," Crothers said when Luis sat down at his desk, "little late today, huh?"

"Rough night, man," Luis said, eyes closed against the

bright lights of the station. "My head's killing me." And it was. Not phantom pain this time, but real and sharp, like someone was reaching into his head with a red-hot poker, singeing the gray matter of his brain.

"Want a Tylenol or something?"

"Nah," Luis said, "I'll make it."

"You say so. Anyway, we got a call. Missing person out on La Cienega. Ready to hit the road?"

"Yeah, let's roll."

By the time they reached the nightclub they were headed for on La Cienega, Luis was in agony. The sun was brutal, glaring in through the windshield and into his eyes like dull knives. He heard a sound and realized that he had moaned. Crothers turned and looked at him.

"You all right, compadre?"

"Your glasses," Luis said, "give me your sunglasses."

Crothers took off his dark shades and handed them to Luis, who fitted them over his eyes. Better, a little better. He laid his head back against the headrest and closed his eyes, tried to clear his head, zone the pain out.

"You coming in, man?" Crothers said, opening his door. "We got a case to work here, you know."

"Can you take this one, Steve?" Luis whispered. "I need a sec."

Crothers blew air out of his nose and slammed the car door. At that moment, Luis could have killed his partner of six years with no compunctions whatsoever.

"Back in a few," Crothers said. Luis heard gravel crunching under his partner's feet as he headed toward the club.

Luis tried to relax. He slumped down in his seat, covered his face with his arm, and stared at the backs of his eyelids, taking deep breaths. But suddenly the backs of his eyelids weren't black anymore, and the air he inhaled was pungent, smelling strongly of cherry blossoms and rain.

Feeling a surge of panic rising in his chest, Luis opened his eyes and jerked into a sitting position.

What he saw scared him more than anything he'd ever seen.

The scene that had been in front of him when he and Crothers arrived at the club was still there, unchanged. The gray cinderblock exterior of the club, a big one called Night-shade, was lit almost white by the sun, which had grown to a brilliant and incendiary brutality as it rose in the sky. The street was nearly empty at this hour, save for a few passers-by. Two men sat in front of the club on the curb, both hobos Luis recognized from working the same neighborhood for so many years. All of that was the same.

The difference was that the scene in front of Luis wasn't all he was seeing. Superimposed over the sunny Los Angeles scenery was an image Luis didn't recognize, and one in motion. More than anything, it was like someone had aimed two movie projectors at the same screen at the same time, only this screen was in Luis' mind.

The alternate scene was darker than the real one, nighttime. The image he was seeing was also of a street, but not one he knew. This one was lined with bushy trees and big houses set back behind substantial front yards. A crescent moon hung low in the sky over the street.

As he watched, breathless, the image moved.

Out of the corner of his eye, Luis saw motion, something bursting from its hiding place behind a shrub perhaps a hundred feet away.

It was a young girl. *Her,* Luis thought, *it's her.*

There was an unbearable stabbing pain in his head.

He woke up sometime later.

He was in a dark place, lying down on his back. Something soft was bunched up underneath his head—his jacket. There were voices, lots of voices, from just a few feet away.

Luis sat up and the pain accosted him, ripped through his skull like rusty barbed wire. He screamed and clamped his hands to his head, palms over his eyes.

"Jesus!" he screamed, "Jesus Christ!"

A door slammed open and someone rushed in. A wedge of bright light tore in from outside.

"Close it!" Luis screamed. "Close the fucking door!"

"Argento, calm down, it's okay." Crothers.

Luis was crying. He couldn't help it, couldn't stop. "Where am I? What happened?"

"When I came back to the car, you were out cold," Crothers said. "I brought you back to the station, put you in the lounge on the couch, and turned off the lights. You've been out for more than an hour, man."

An hour. He couldn't remember anything. What the hell was happening?

Luis stood up and a fresh wave of agony flooded his skull. He barely managed to hold in another scream.

"I have to go," he said, pulling his jacket on. He yanked open the door and stumbled out of the lounge, leaving Crothers standing in the darkness.

Instinct rather than sight guided him to his car. He fell into the black Mustang and popped the glove-box open, then fumbled through the maps and papers until he found an old pair of shades. One of the lenses was cracked, but he put them on anyway. Anything to lessen the pain that was threatening once again to rob him of his senses. All he could think of was getting home and into bed, where it was dark and cool.

He started the car and pulled out of the lot onto La Cruz Boulevard, almost sideswiping a passing Beemer.

The pain was suddenly gone, leaving only numbness in its wake.

It was at least ten seconds before Luis remembered to breathe again.

He touched his fingers to his temples, driving with one hand. In a single second he felt incredible relief that the pain was gone, and incredible fear that the pain had abated because something inside his brain had finally given way, and that even as he sat in relieved painlessness, the cavities of his skull were flooding with blood. He stopped at a red light and waited for it to turn. Finally it did and he continued on down La Cruz, heading east toward La Brea.

When he reached the red light at the intersection, he flicked on his left blinker and moved into the turn lane.

Pain erupted in his head, igniting blossoms of red fire in the spaces behind his eyes, which pulsed sadistically with every click of the turn signal. "No!" he screamed, "God, no please!" A flailing hand hit the blinker-arm and disengaged it, and just as suddenly as it had come upon him, the pain was gone again.

Luis sat in stunned silence, panting and sweating. He didn't see the left-turn arrow switch to green, and the horn of the car behind him blared, snapping him from his stupor. Glancing in the rearview mirror, Luis merged back into the eastbound lane.

When he hit Fifth Avenue, he tried to turn again, right this time, but before he even reached to put on his blinker, he felt the fire start in the front of his brain.

So he continued east.

By the time he reached the entrance for Interstate 10 in Monterey Park, his mind was made up. He flicked on his blinker and merged into traffic for eastbound 10, and this time there was no pain.

Chapter 4

Cole woke up and lay still, letting the tears make their way down the sides of his face and onto his pillow. After a moment he turned his head to look at the alarm clock on his bedside table. It read 11:38 p.m.

God, he thought. *An hour. I can't even get an hour's worth of sleep anymore.*

He swung his legs over the side of the bed and stood, then pulled on the crimson bathrobe that lay draped over the chair in the corner of the bedroom.

Wiping the last of the moisture from his eyes with the sleeve of the bathrobe, Cole went into the kitchen and filled the silver kettle with water, then set it to boil on the stove. When it was hot, he took a mug from the cabinet and brewed himself some chamomile tea.

The living room of his apartment was sparsely furnished, populated only by a small sofa and a couple of chairs in the alcove that overlooked the water. Sometimes it was hard for him to believe he'd once had a life other than this one. A son, a wife, a house. But that was all gone now. It had been for a long time.

Taking his tea, he sat in one of the chairs by the window and put his feet up on the sill.

He pressed his bare feet against the glass of the window and felt the cold radiating through. It looked like another rough night out there. Snow was coming down, not particularly fast, but heavy, the way it does in Maine. *At this rate,* he thought, *they'd have another foot by sun-up.*

When he'd first arrived in Maine, the snow had irritated him, but the longer he lived with it, the more he'd come to enjoy it. It wasn't as though he had to drive to work anyway. The dock was just a block and a half down Main Street, easily hikable, even in the most inclement weather. His old Honda Civic hadn't moved from its spot at the curb for a good month, at least. Cole didn't get out much. Everything he needed he could get in town.

He looked out over the bay and saw the lighthouse beam on the island come around, a flicker of light in the snowy, shifting darkness, then move on.

Though he tried to avoid it, his thoughts inevitably returned to the dream he'd woken from. The dream, the fucking dream. He'd never been woken by it this early before, but then, things had been different again, so all bets were off.

As with the previous version, this night's dream had progressed according to the actual events of the day of Jimmy's death, only this time there were two changes from the orig- . inal.

Pushing into the center of the circle of people that had formed around his wife and son, Cole had looked down and seen Cora lying prone on the grass, not Jimmy, and though that had come to be expected to his waking self, it was still a terrible shock to his somnambulant one.

What he hadn't anticipated, though, either in his waking or sleeping life, was seeing the woman who was now cradling Cora's head in her lap.

It was no longer his wife. Now it was Sarah Delacort.

Chapter 5

At around midnight, Luis pulled off Route 15 into a rest stop just outside Cedar City, Utah. His eyes were blurred with sleep, and he'd already drifted off once, only to wake up moments later in the oncoming lane, shocked out of sleep by the rumble strip on the far side of the thankfully deserted highway.

The landscape all around him was white with a powdery layer of snow, a shocking departure from the sun-drenched vistas through which he'd been driving all afternoon. The change had come as he passed through the mountains beyond Las Vegas that formed the northeastern border of the Mojave Desert. Summer on one side, winter on the other. It only added to the disorientation Luis already felt.

There were no other cars in sight, so Luis pulled up outside the blocky structure that housed the restrooms and vending machines and turned the car off.

After making sure that all the doors were locked, he slumped down behind the wheel and closed his eyes, exhausted, looking forward to his first sleep in two weeks that wouldn't be plagued by headaches.

He pulled his jacket more tightly around himself and tucked his hands underneath his armpits, then surrendered himself to fatigue. But his mind, though heavily taxed by the day's events, wasn't ready to sleep yet. As they had for most of the day, his thoughts remained on the image of the girl from the vision he'd had outside the nightclub that afternoon.

Seeing her had been a shock, the last thing he'd expected. Not to say that he didn't recognize her, because he did, but he hadn't consciously thought of her in weeks. Only now did he realize how close to his thoughts she'd remained all this time.

Luis clearly remembered the first time he'd seen the girl. He'd been on the prowl in Beverly Hills, not his usual hunting grounds, but that was exactly the point. He knew through departmental gossip that his MO was becoming well known in West Hollywood, where he usually trolled for prey, so he'd expanded his territory and headed for less familiar ground.

He'd encountered the girl and her family outside a Thai restaurant where they'd apparently dined. Though something had instantly attracted him to the family, the girl wasn't the first member he'd noticed.

The girl's mother had been beautiful, a real knockout, maybe forty but still fit and athletic-looking in khaki shorts and a black T-shirt. She wore her blond hair long and over her shoulders, which were brown with tan and a smattering of tiny freckles, just enough to make the mind wonder whether she was freckled everywhere. Her father was attractive also, well built and sturdy-looking in his chinos and white button-down. His hair was brown, but going salt and pepper at the temples. He looked like he was in good shape, too. As Luis always did when encountering another male for the first time, he wondered how difficult it would be to take the man down. As he would discover just a short while later, the answer was: *not very.*

Though his first instinct was to stop and stare at the family, Luis hadn't wanted to attract undue attention to himself, so he'd kept on walking, stopping a safe distance away to take another look.

And that's when he'd seen the girl.

He hadn't noticed her at first, since she'd been standing behind her mother, but when she came into his view, he was instantly captivated. She was angelic, perfect. He watched as she took her little brother's hand in her own and started down the sidewalk behind her parents, heading his way.

As they passed him by, he'd been unable to help himself and looked at her, anxious to see if she was as flawless up close as she was from afar.

He'd found her looking directly at him, a puzzled look on her face. When their eyes met, she didn't look away, as would most girls her age, but rather smiled at him, and he'd heard a gentle, indistinct murmuring in his head, something he could almost understand, but not quite. Like words spoken low on a windy day, he could hear the music, but not the meaning.

Compelled, and already feeling the first threads of fear working their way into his thoughts, he'd dropped a safe distance behind and followed.

Luis knew the area well, so it wasn't hard to keep track of them as they went in and out of stores, which they did repeatedly. When they made the turn onto Rodeo Drive, his job was made even simpler. Most of the stores along Rodeo's main strip were small boutiques with only one entrance, so he could wait for the family to reemerge as he sat on a bench, looking like just one more tired husband patiently waiting for his wife to finish shopping.

It was during one such episode that Luis' first instincts about the girl were reaffirmed.

When the family came out of the store they'd been in for some time—Luis thought it might have been Tiffany's but couldn't recall well enough now to be sure—the girl had been in the lead, holding her father's hand. The second she stepped out onto the sidewalk, it was as if she smelled Luis. The smile on her face faded and was replaced by a darker look, a fearful one. Her head snapped in his direction, and her eyes fixed on him where he was sitting, perhaps a hundred feet away. He'd wanted to look away from her, but had found himself unable to do so. Her eyes were like powerful magnets and held him fast.

Then, as quickly as she'd snared him, she let him go again and Luis actually reeled back on the bench, like a drunk trying to keep his balance. When he could, Luis looked back in the girl's direction and saw her talking to her father, pointing in his direction.

Standing, he'd made his way through the flow of human traffic and into a clothing shop on the other side of the sidewalk. He didn't want to lose the family, but neither did he want the parents to become too suspicious and worried. If that happened, they might do something unpredictable, like call a cab, or even worse, the police. No doubt, the mother and father both had cell phones, so help was only a few button-pushes away at any moment. Better to drop off for a while and let them reassure the girl.

After a few minutes of pretending to browse through the racks of clothing, Luis left the shop.

The family was nowhere to be seen. Luis thought for a moment, then turned left down the sidewalk and started walking, continuing in the same direction the family had been going all afternoon. There weren't many more shops down this way, but there were two parking garages, and Luis was guessing the family had had just about all the shopping they could stand for one day.

He started off at a fast walk, but soon found himself running, dodging oncoming pedestrians as he navigated his way along the crowded sidewalk.

Where were they? He hadn't been in the clothing shop for that long; they couldn't have gotten too far ahead. Had he made the wrong choice? Was the family parked somewhere in the other direction?

For the first time he realized just how worried he was about losing the girl. The way she'd looked at him . . . twice, like she knew something, like she'd felt something. And that soft noise he'd heard when she and her family passed him the first time, that noise like whispering in his head, her whispering. Could she have seen inside of him, inside his mind? Was that possible? Whether or not it was, he only knew that he felt it was true. If she got away from him, he would never feel safe, the way he always had. Her existence would haunt him. Somehow, the possibility that someone could know about the things he'd done made them worse. What if that whispering had been the sound of her reading his thoughts? The sound of that murmuring, like a gently lilting tell-tale heart in his head, a sound so low you had to listen, really listen, to hear what it was saying. Even now he could hear it . . .

He caught up with them outside the first of the two parking garages. On the other side of the street, the parents were leading their children toward the door to the garage's stairs.

Slowing to a walk, Luis became aware that people were staring at him. He could understand why. A grown man dressed in a suit, running down the sidewalk, sweat pouring off his face like a marathon racer. Not something you saw everyday in Beverly Hills, land of the slow and casual. He wiped his forehead with a hand and brushed the sweat off on the leg of his pants, leaving a wet smear on the dark blue fabric, then straightened his tie and ran his hands over his short, black hair, slicking it back. Better.

The girl and her family were stepping into the stairwell of the parking garage on the other side of the street. As Luis crossed over, he concentrated on slowing his breathing, gathering himself.

Stepping inside the narrow stairwell, Luis slipped his hand into his pocket and caressed the smooth grip of the straight razor. He took the stairs two at a time; from above he could hear the children talking and laughing, the parents chiming in with their own laughter. As he rounded the corner and stepped onto the landing between the fourth and fifth floors of the garage, he saw the mother stepping through the exit door. Before it could swing all the way shut, he vaulted up the remaining stairs and eased through, pulling the razor out of his pocket. A quick look in both directions told him what he already sensed; they were alone.

What he remembered from there on was a bit of a blur, as it always was. All he ever retained from his killings was a rough recollection, more an outline of events than anything else. He'd heard that some predators recalled everything about their kills in minute, exact detail and pored over those memories again and again, but it had never been that way for Luis. Sometimes he could remember almost nothing, which was why he'd started photographing his victims. Sometimes his snapshots helped spark a memory, but with the girl's family there had been no pictures.

What he remembered was that he came in from behind and killed the father first with a slash of the razor across the side of the neck, dropping him fast. He did the mother next, and then the brother, not taking the time he would have liked with any of them. He was accustomed to working in private, in the security of his own home, and every moment he lingered out where someone might see him was an unwanted risk, an uncomfortable aberration from a time-tested routine.

When he was finished with the rest of the family, he found that the girl had run. He chased her through the streets behind the parking garage, dropping and regaining her trail a number of times, before losing her for good. He had a feeling she'd gone to ground, but the thought that she might have found a phone and called the police scared him enough that he'd eventually been forced to abandon his search.

Ever since that day, Luis had felt somehow lost, incomplete. It wasn't simply that he'd let the girl get away; it was as though she'd taken a part of him with her, a vital part, and without it—without it he felt like half the man he'd been, less than that, even. God, he was tired. So tired. Outside the car, the wind blew hard, rocking the car gently. His thoughts were slowing down, and Luis was conscious of his sinking toward—

The vision took Luis suddenly, sucking him down and in.

Again, it was like he was seeing through the eyes of someone else, only the image was much sharper, set as it was against the darkness afforded by his closed eyes instead of the brightness of daytime Los Angeles.

The first time this had happened, Luis had been taken by surprise, and that, coupled with his concerns about the headaches, had made him fearful, but now he let himself be drawn in. That his dreams and headaches were somehow linked to these visions was obvious, and Luis wanted to understand how.

Like before, the setting of the scene was a deserted nighttime street. To his right was a copse of tall trees, and beyond those, the roofs of several houses, with black shingles and red brick chimneys.

In the distance, a church steeple was visible, lit from below by bright lights. There was a clock mounted on each face of the towering spire, but the church was far enough away that Luis couldn't see what time their faces read.

He panned his gaze slowly, searching the night for movement. To his immediate right was a white sign with black letters, lit from within. It said: BRIDGEWATER INN. On the other side of a large parking lot, the structure itself was bulked in shadow. There were no lights on in the building, and the parking lot was empty. Like everything else Luis had seen so far, both in this vision and the first, it was deserted. He wondered where this place was, and where all the people were.

He walked slowly through the parking lot and into the Inn's lobby, scanning the area quickly but attentively.

When a quick search of the office proved uneventful, he turned and left, heading quickly across the parking lot for the outdoor stairs leading to the second floor of the structure. At the top, he turned right and walked to the first of maybe fifteen doors that ran the length of the building. Reaching down with a black-gloved hand, he jiggled the knob, and, finding the door locked, drew back a foot to kick it in.

At that moment, a flurry of motion caught his eye.

On the other end of the covered walkway that ran the length of the second floor, the door to one of the rooms opened and the girl emerged, dressed in dark clothing. She was too far away to get a very good look, but Luis was sure it was the same girl. The same girl he'd lost in Los Angeles and the same girl he'd seen in his earlier vision. Without a backward glance, she turned and fled down the stairway on the other side of the walkway, gracefully taking the stairs four and five at a time.

Luis instantly made chase but, instead of taking the stairs back down to the ground, he placed one hand on the black railing and simply vaulted over, falling the twelve or so feet to the earth. He landed softly, and then was off, headed after the girl.

She had run through the parking lot and straight across the street on the other side, then down a shadowy road covered by a thick canopy of trees.

Luis ran down the middle of the street, keeping his eyes on the fleet form perhaps a hundred feet in front of him. Through a gap in the trees overhead, Luis noticed the steeple of the church he'd seen before was getting closer, and then, suddenly, the canopy ended and he found himself standing at the outskirts of a small downtown district.

Stretching off to the right was a row of stores with different colored awnings, mostly blue and dark green. To the left was a playground; a squeaking sound drew his eyes there, but it was only the sound of a merry-go-round blowing slowly in a circle.

Somehow, he'd lost sight of the girl, but the soft jingling of bells started him in the direction of the stores to the right.

The first one he passed was a Laundromat. Luis peered in the large window but saw no movement and no place to hide. He moved on.

Next was a hardware store. He reached for the door-handle before seeing the padlock affixed to the clasp at head-level. Not in there.

The name printed on the blue awning of the next store was *T. Bumbles*. The display in the window was of a beach scene, with a red plastic bucket full of sand standing lopsided in a gigantic heap of the yellowish-white stuff. Foil had been laid out to resemble the ocean, and the "beach" was littered with toy spades and rakes, as well as a generous smattering of seashells and rocks, some big as tennis balls and some small enough to be called pebbles. The back of the display was a wall-to-wall piece of poster board, painted powder blue with small white clouds and a yellow sun in the corner.

Luis reached down and tried the handle, but the door wouldn't budge. Locked.

Something caught Luis' eye as he was about to move on. Four sleigh bells on a thick leather strip hung from the top of the door. *Ah,* Luis thought.

The door itself was a pane of glass framed by wood. Luis drew back his hand and rammed it through, punching a hole in the glass near the door handle. After a second, his searching fingers found the deadbolt on the other side of the door and twisted it.

He pulled the door open and stepped inside the store.

It was even darker inside than outside. Luis didn't bother searching for a light switch; he knew somehow that the lights wouldn't work. Not here, not anywhere in this odd town.

Reaching back with one hand, Luis locked the door again, then dug his hand into his hip pocket. When he pulled it back out, he was holding his razor tightly in his fist.

The store was square in shape and fairly small, no more than twenty feet long and about as wide. The middle was mostly taken up by a large island that supported a wooden shelf of brightly-colored stuffed animals and action figures. There weren't many hiding places.

Back door, Luis thought. *She's gone for the back door.*

He headed for the rear of the store. A rainbow curtain of hanging beads separated the store from the office area in back. He pushed through and emerged into the small space, which was dominated by a large desk and two file cabinets.

The back door was shut and locked. In addition to the lock on the doorknob, there were two clasps meant for padlocks.

Both were engaged, and a Masterlock hung loosely from one. If she had come in here, she hadn't left through this door. Luis reached up and engaged the lock.

From out in the main room, there was a thunk as something was knocked over.

He pushed back through the beads and surveyed the darkened store.

There was no movement, but Luis could practically feel the tension in the room. She was still here.

With a slow and deliberate motion, Luis flicked his wrist, and the straight razor in his hand swung open.

Listening intently, he moved farther into the store, searching for his prey.

With a swipe of his right arm, Luis knocked over a heap of stuffed koala bears piled on the knee-high shelf that circled the store. A rotating rack of greeting cards partially obscured his view of the corner, so he sent that flying, too, spilling stationery all over the floor.

There was another sound, coming from somewhere close to the front of the store, near the door. Luis suddenly realized where the girl was, and moved in a line toward the store's display window.

As he closed in, Luis began to experience the familiar thrumming in his brain, though his veins. He could feel the razor slicing through her flesh, scraping on bone. It was only a matter of time now, inevitable.

He reached the back of the window display and, with a slash of the razor, cut through the poster board, then fit a hand into the gash and pulled, ripping it down.

The girl came at him with her hand raised, as if to strike.

Luis stood unafraid, content to let her come to him. She threw her hand out toward his head, and it was only when Luis' eyes erupted in a bonfire of agony that he realized that she hadn't been striking out at him, but that she'd tossed something in his face.

There was a crash as something heavy went through the display window, probably one of the bigger rocks, and then the crunching of broken glass as the girl hopped down to the sidewalk and fled.

Luis snapped free of the vision as quickly as he had been sucked into it, digging at his eyes with clawed fingers. When he tried to open his eyes, he was rewarded with a fresh wave of pain, and could see only the blurred outlines of things, just enough to be certain that he was free of the vision, back in his own body.

With a desperate hand he fumbled for the car's door-handle, screaming in frustration and pain when he found it locked.

Managing at last to escape the vehicle, he made his way as quickly as he could into the building that housed the restrooms.

There was a water fountain between the men's and the women's rooms, and he pushed the button, dropping his face into the high arc of cold water.

When he thought he'd be able to do so, he opened his eyes and let the water flush them out as well. After two or three minutes, he stood up and wiped wet hair back from his forehead.

"Bitch," he said, moaning at the remembrance of pain, "that little bitch."

His thirst for blood unfulfilled, Luis was super-alert and on edge. How he'd wanted to cover his hands in her blood! How he'd wanted to cut her until she was nothing more than a mass of unrecognizable parts!

From outside the building there was a bang, the slamming of a car door. Luis looked out through the window and saw a young man dressed in worn jeans, a heavy flannel shirt, and an orange goosedown vest walking up the path, most likely to use the restroom.

When the kid entered, Luis took two long steps toward him, as though headed for the door to leave, and cut the punk's throat with one slash, dropping him to the ground, where he got on with the slow business of staining the floor red.

He wiped the blood from his razor and pocketed it, then drew his Glock and left the building.

Parked next to his Mustang was a green Jeep Wrangler.

Sitting in the passenger seat was a pretty blond girl, eighteen or nineteen, same as the kid from inside. The little fucker's whore. She was putting on an offensively red shade of lipstick, checking herself out in the mirror on the backside of the lowered sun-guard.

She was oblivious to Luis' approach, so when he arrived, he tapped twice lightly on the window with the barrel of his gun.

When she looked, obviously expecting her boyfriend, he pumped six rounds into her head and chest. Now the lipstick was the dullest shade of red she wore.

Feeling slightly more calm, Luis reholstered his gun and got into his car, not tired anymore, feeling remarkably refreshed, in fact, as though he could drive all night.

Chapter 6

Sarah Delacort drove into Stone Beach from the south, having taken the Coastal Route up most of the way from Boston. Her first thought was that it was a funny little fishing town, like the countless other funny little fishing towns she'd driven through during her trip up Route 1. The only place she'd seen that reminded her even remotely of real civilization was Freeport, and that was upon her and then gone again in five forgettable minutes.

The downtown area of Stone Beach consisted of around fifteen to twenty storefronts, lined up one after the other along a quarter-mile stretch of the snowy highway, all facing the ocean, separated from its gray waters only by a road, a sidewalk, and the Stone Beach Marina. At least five of the stores were bars, or Sarah assumed they were from the numerous neon beer signs hanging in their windows and the names on their tired-looking awnings—The Salty Dog, Lou's, The Stone Beach Pub, Hair of the Dog, and the Backstretch. There was also what looked like a general store, the only place that seemed to be doing any business, two hardware stores, and a little barbershop, complete with a red-and-white peppermint stick mounted outside the door.

Sarah pulled her rental, a hunter green Lexus sedan, over to the curb outside the Backstretch, which looked like the classiest bar of the bunch, and climbed out, unfolding her long legs from underneath the dash with a stiff groan.

The clean smell of saltwater and snow slapped her coldly in the face and she reached her hands up in a full-out stretch, extending her slender body as far as it would go, sucking in a deep, lung-popping breath. It was the cleanest air she'd smelled in years, since before leaving North Carolina for Philadelphia.

Inside the bar it was dark. Five or six men sat drinking, hunched tiredly on their stools, elbows resting on the dull surface of the wood bar. Every one of them looked up at her appraisingly when she entered, and their eyes stayed on her as she approached the bar.

The bartender, a short man with a hanging gut and a truly bad combover, was busy drying glasses that didn't look very clean with a white rag, then setting them back on their shelves. He had to perch up on his tiptoes to reach the top-most shelves.

"Excuse me," Sarah said, "can you tell me where Haverhill House is?"

The bartender slid a glass onto a manageably low shelf and then walked over to her, wiping his hands dry on the rag. He had ruddy skin and a ragged goatee, much fuller on one side than the other. Sarah felt off-balance just looking at him.

"You stayin' there?" he said. Sarah could feel his eyes on her breasts and felt dirty from it, could picture in her mind what he was picturing in his.

"Not yet," Sarah said, pulling her coat more tightly around herself, the courteous smile fading rapidly from her lips, "but I'd like to be sometime soon."

He grinned and set both hands on the bar, leaning forward. "Why don't you stick around here for dinner, then I'll show you where Haverhill House is myself when I get off."

Sarah rolled her eyes discreetly. She had what she'd come in for, anyway.

"Up Main Street two more blocks then left up the hill on Walnut, you say? Great, thanks." She turned and headed for the door, leaving the confused bartender to stare at her retreating back, though it was more likely her ass he was catching an eyeful of. As the door was easing shut behind her, she heard the bartender call out, "If you knew where the fucking thing was to begin with, then why the hell did you ask?"

Haverhill House was charming, just as Cole had said it would be. Not exactly the Ritz, but charming nonetheless. It was a large white Victorian with castle-like turrets on either side of the façade and a wrap-around porch boasting white wicker lawn chairs, though Sarah thought it was about fifty degrees too cold to make any good use of those.

Inside, Sarah found a tidy-looking older man wearing gray slacks and a blue cashmere sweater sitting behind the service desk. He showed her to her room on the second floor, even carrying her suitcase up the stairs for her.

The room itself was small, just the bedroom and an adjoining bathroom, but impeccably clean. A tall window to the left of the old four-poster bed overlooked the ocean.

Sarah glanced at the alarm clock and saw that she still had a couple of hours till dinner, so she showered and then lay down for a catnap, wrapped in one of the house's huge, fuzzy white towels.

The phone woke her and she snapped it up, awake instantly. "Hello?"

"Sarah? It's me, Cole."

"Cole." For a moment she was confused. Though awake, her mind hadn't fully processed the events of the past couple days, and the very first thing she felt at hearing Cole's voice was relief, and her first thought, Oh, thank God, I had a terrible dream that you'd left . . .

And then, as fast as she could draw a breath, she remembered where she was, what day and year it was, and why she was there.

"Cole. How are you?"

"Good," he answered. "It's good to hear your voice again."

"Yours, too."

There was a long silence, and then Cole spoke again. "Dinner? I know a great place."

"Sure," she said. "When?"

"Half an hour?"

"Okay."

"I'll pick you up," he said. "See you soon." There was a click and Sarah set the receiver back on its cradle.

She dressed in jeans and a white, long-sleeved button-down, then pulled on a pair of heavy, black leather boots, real ass-kickers, a remnant from her misguided youth. Cole hadn't said what kind of place it was they were going to; she hoped what she was wearing looked okay.

Hand on the doorknob, Sarah stopped. Something wasn't right, something was missing. Following a feeling she didn't entirely understand, she turned away from the door and crouched beside her suitcase, opened the zipper to one of the inside pockets, reached in, and pulled out a silver barrette.

"Huh," she said, turning it over in her hands. The barrette was adorned with three silver flowers in a row. It was heavy, which she'd always liked, she remembered, not like those flimsy plastic ones you could buy for a buck a dozen.

But how had it gotten in her suitcase? She hadn't seen the old thing in . . . well, in years. "Oh, what the hell," she muttered, standing up.

She pulled her hair back into a ponytail and used the barrette to secure it, liking the feeling of that old weight, then left her room and headed down to meet Cole.

He pulled up outside the Haverhill House a few minutes later in an old Honda Civic. Or she assumed it was him, at any rate. It was frigid outdoors, and the windows of the car were fogged on the inside, so she couldn't see the driver. A jet of gray plumed from the car's exhaust pipe as the old engine rattled away.

Standing inside the house, looking out the window beside the front door, Sarah could no longer deny that she was terrified. Man, she thought, get a grip. The worst that's going to happen is that he'll be fat and bald and completely uninterested.

There was a tap on her shoulder and she nearly jumped out of her skin, just managing to hold back a scream. She turned around and saw the old man who had helped her with her bags earlier.

He smiled at her. "I know it's cold," he said, "but the sooner you go, the sooner you'll get there."

"Right," she said, returning the smile. "Thanks." Taking a deep breath, she opened the door of the house, stepped out onto the porch, and hurried down to the car. The door was pushed open as she approached, and reaching the car, she plunged in, pulling the door shut behind her.

For a moment, all she could do was look at her hands, though she could feel his eyes on her. Her sprint down to the car had left her short of breath, though she thought that was only part of the reason her chest felt oddly tight.

Her heart felt like it was beating every tenth of a second, in direct contradiction to the laws of nature, and she felt herself flushing badly. She hoped he would recognize it as a consequence of her run, and not for what it really was.

Forcing herself to raise her head, she looked at Cole Johnstone for the first time in nearly ten years.

He looked almost exactly the same as he had in med school, during their brief life together. His brown hair was showing the first hints of gray around the sideburns, and there was a smattering of tiny wrinkles near the edges of his eyes and mouth, but he still looked young, boyish. "Long time," she said.

"You look really great, Sarah," Cole said, and though she thought he meant it, she still felt bizarrely self-conscious, aware of how ridiculous she must look to him, dressed in her college girl wardrobe.

She ran a hand back over her hair, smoothing it, only half realizing what she was doing with the motion. "Thanks," she said, "you do, too."

There was a silence; then he spoke, breaking it. "You still have that old thing," he said.

"What?"

"That." He pointed at her head and she raised a hand to her ponytail and touched the silver barrette.

"Oh," she said, feigning surprise, "right. I didn't even realize I was wearing it."

He was quiet for a second. "I think that was the first thing I ever gave you."

She smiled back, then quipped, "Cole, I think this is the only thing you ever gave me."

"Yeah? Well, that's my own stupid fault, I guess." His eyes met hers and stayed. "Hey," he said, "come here." He parted his arms and she leaned forward and wrapped her own around him, leaning her head against his shoulder. They held each other tightly for a few seconds, then let go.

"It's really good to see you again," he said, leaning back into his seat.

Sarah nodded back. "It's nice for me, too." She waited a second, then said gravely, "Cole, there's something I really have to tell you, something you need to know."

"What is it?" He looked concerned.

"I don't have much time left."

"What?" he said. "Are you all right?"

"No," she said, "no, I'm not. If I don't get some dinner soon, I'm going to eat my own goddamned foot. Take me to food."

The concerned look fled from his face and was replaced by a wide grin. "You shit," he said, laughing. "You scared the bejeesus out of me, Sarah."

He took her to dinner at a little place called Donovan's in the next town. It overlooked the water and the warm odors of bread and pasta were somehow intoxicating when combined with the cold, salty air that blew in every time someone opened the door.

Sarah ordered linguine in a thick Alfredo sauce with shrimp and lobster and red and orange sliced peppers. She dug in as soon as it arrived. It was minutes before she glanced up and saw Cole looking at her.

"What?" she said through a mouthful of pasta, wiping her lips with her napkin.

"You still eat like a Viking," he said, grinning, dabbing at his own mouth with his napkin.

She smiled and sipped her wine, a pleasingly sweet white. "Benefit of four older brothers."

"Yeah," Cole said, "I remember. None of them liked me much."

"And that was before you dumped me. If any of them saw you now, they'd murder you."

"With good reason, too. I was a prick."

"You said it, not me."

67

Cole grinned sheepishly. "I see time hasn't dulled your knack for brutal honesty."

"Like they say," Sarah said, with eyebrow arched, "some things never change."

"But some things do," he countered. "For instance, you have become remarkably successful, Sarah Delacort. When last our paths crossed, you were just a confused kid, and now you're just about the only psychic in the world the mention of whose name doesn't beckon a chorus of laughter."

"Thank you," she said, sipping again from her glass, enjoying both the pleasing taste of the wine and the warm fuzziness it was slowly causing inside her body, "for that ringing endorsement."

"You know what I mean."

She nodded slowly. "Things have changed for you, too."

He shrugged and dropped his eyes, becoming pensive. "Things were good, and then they weren't so good anymore." He spun his fork in his spaghetti, but didn't raise it to his mouth.

Sarah felt like an ass. She had no idea what had so rapidly changed his mood, but felt as though she should have, the way she always felt when she failed to read people's signs properly.

"I'm sorry," she murmured. "Did I say something terrible?" She sensed an almost overwhelming sadness about him, and though she could have known more in a second if she'd wanted to, she didn't. It had taken a long time and a lot of training to get to the point where she could learn, or in this case re-learn, about someone slowly, and that was almost always how she chose to do things now.

She was torn between trying to swing the conversation in a less personal direction and trying to get to the heart of the problem. In the end she chose the latter. "Are you still married to that little blond thing you left me for?" she said, trying to keep her voice as light and jocular as she could. "What was her name, Jessica?"

"No," Cole said, "not for five years now. She's back in North Carolina."

"What happened?"

Cole chuckled softly and drank some wine, some of the previous spirit back in his eyes. "I guess she just decided that she'd rather be married to an old prof at Duke than to a young doctor with a so-so gig at some shitty clinic in Maine. It actually makes pretty good sense, if you think about it."

"She married one the profs at the medical school?"

Cole leaned forward and said conspiratorially, "Yeah, and it was that ugly bastard Harding, too." He laughed, then said, "I was pretty upset for a few months, until I decided that having to sleep with that dog-faced fatso was punishment enough in itself. Anyway, I hope she's happy." Cole laughed again and this time Sarah joined him. It wasn't his ex he was sad about, she decided, it was something else entirely.

Suddenly the image of a child, young, maybe three or four and blond-haired, dressed in coveralls and a red T-shirt, flashed into her mind and then was gone just as quickly as it had come, a powerful but fleeting impression. What did that mean? Had it come from Cole or someone else in the restaurant?

He was saying her name.

"Hmm? What?"

"I said, are you married?"

"Oh, no. Never. Managed to dodge that bullet a few times." The picture of the child was still with her, like the powerful after-image the sun leaves on your cornea after a direct glance. Wide smile, freckles on his cheeks, achingly beautiful brown eyes, familiar eyes.

Sarah shook her head once, trying to get rid of the impression.

"You okay?" Cole said.

"Fine," Sarah replied, "just a little tired. Why don't you tell me about this girl you're so anxious for me to see?"

"Cora Gardner."

"Yes."

Cole told her about Cora's condition, the RN's disappearance, and the various strange sightings on the island the past couple of weeks.

"And . . . you think what, exactly?" Sarah said, sensing that there was something Cole wanted to say, but was afraid to for some reason.

A pained look came over his face. Sarah knew instantly that he was in some kind of conflict about whatever it was he was withholding.

"It's okay, Cole, you can tell me if you can tell anyone. I'm a loony psychic, remember?"

"Okay," he said, his voice dropping as though he didn't want anyone to overhear what he was going to tell her. "I don't think Cora is in a coma, at least not in the conventional sense."

Sarah was confused. "But didn't you just say that she's been unconscious for over two weeks?"

"I'm not sure 'unconscious' is the right word. Her eyes have been closed and it sure looks like she's unconscious, but for most of every day her EEG records brain patterns typical of someone who is awake."

"And that means what?"

He shook his head. "I'm not sure, but when you look at the history of her case, it's hard not to think that something really odd is going on."

"What do you mean? What's so odd?"

"For one, there was no physical trauma." He paused and then said, "Or at least there wasn't when she was admitted."

"Was there an accident in the Clinic?"

"No." Cole shook his head. "No accident, but from time to time small cuts and bruises show up on her arms and legs, cause unknown. Once, about a week and a half ago, the nurse bathing her found a bruise the size of a grapefruit on her ribcage, and then yesterday I noticed some swelling in her hand. Turns out three of her fingers were broken. And I mean really broken. Someone crushed the hell out of them."

Sarah thought for a second. "Spontaneous bruising has been known to happen, if only rarely, but cuts and broken bones? Man."

Cole nodded, effectively echoing the sentiment.

She filed the data away for further consideration later. "What else?"

"Well," Cole said, "since there was no trauma, the coma, or whatever it is, would appear to be shock-induced, maybe the effect of post-traumatic stress."

Sarah finished off the rest of the wine in her glass and poured herself some more, then looked at Cole, who nodded. She emptied the bottle into his glass.

"What reason would she have for retreating into a coma-tose state? Did something happen that could have triggered her?" Sarah leaned back in her chair and crossed her legs. She could tell from Cole's tone of voice and posture how invested he was in this girl's case and wondered why it was so impor-tant to him.

"Yeah, something most certainly happened," Cole said. "The day she went into the coma, her mother and father and little brother were killed while the three of them were walking to their car in a parking garage in Beverly Hills."

"Car accident?"

Cole shook his head. "Murdered. They were ripped apart by some lunatic with a knife. She was the only one who got away."

"Jesus Christ."

"Yeah," Cole said, "the police found her hiding underneath a car in an alley a couple miles from where the bodies were found. They thought the killer probably missed her at first, then chased her and lost her. Pretty unbelievable, huh?"

"Poor girl. You're right, that sounds like a classic case of post-traumatic stress syndrome. Is there anything else I should know?" she asked, still processing what he'd told her already.

He grinned and nodded. "One more thing. Just after her thirteenth birthday, her father checked her into the Gilleti Institute for a month. Said she was having terrible headaches . . . and that strange things had been happening around the house and at school."

"The Gilleti Institute?" Sarah said. "The one Carmine Gilleti runs in New York?"

"That's the one," Cole said.

"They thought she was psychic?"

Cole nodded. "They thought something was going on, anyway."

Now it was Sarah's turn to smile. "So that's why you wanted me. Why didn't you tell me over the phone?"

Cole shrugged. "Maybe I just wanted to see your face when I laid it on you."

Sarah laughed. "Was it worth the wait?"

"Every second of it."

Chapter 7

The hotel room was like a tomb, tiny and oppressive, with its yellowing wallpaper and brown-stained carpet.

Luis paced, sat down on the narrow bed, got up, and kept on pacing. Movement, movement, he couldn't sit still, not for a minute, not for a second. He felt like he was about to walk right out of his skin, like there was a fish hook through the front of his brain, tugging, tugging.

He looked at the clock: 12:46 a.m.

Questions rushed through his head in a confused whirlwind. *What's happening to me? What am I doing? What's wrong with me? Where am I going?*

The last question was the only one he seemed on his way to an answer with.

All day he'd driven east, stopping only for gas and food, speed steady at sixty-five, pounding out miles, eating the road up. No thought had gone into the day's navigation. One moment he'd be cruising right along, and the next he'd turn off one road and onto another. Simple as pie and, best of all, no pain in his head. But now, now, in this room, the questions came. He had to get out.

He left the hotel and walked next door to the all-night diner, TJ's, stopping on his way in at a pay phone to make a call.

Crothers answered on the first ring.

"Steve," he said, "it's me, Luis."

"Hey, Argento, howya feeling?" Luis could hear Crothers chewing and could imagine him sitting in an old La-Z-Boy in his boxer shorts, eating a TV dinner and drinking a warm Schlitz.

"Not so good," Luis said, keeping his voice low, "that's why I'm calling. Do me a favor and tell Danielson I won't be in tomorrow, okay?"

"Sure, man, no problem. You want me to come by or anything?"

"No," Luis said, "that's okay. I think I just need a little time to get over this."

"All right, but let me know if you need anything."

"Thanks." Luis hung up the phone and went into the diner.

It was all but empty inside. Luis sat at the bar facing the kitchen and ordered coffee and pancakes. He wasn't really hungry but couldn't stand the thought of going back to his room.

An hour later, stomach full enough to be uncomfortable, Luis found that he really was tired, at least enough that he thought he'd be able to fall asleep. He paid his bill and headed back to the hotel, but by the time he got to his room and lay down, he found he was no longer tired at all. His skin felt as though it were on fire, as did his brain, like it had been soaked in gasoline and set alight. The constant feeling of emptiness he'd been feeling was back, and it gnawed at his midsection. It was as though his gastric fluids had been replaced with hydrochloric acid; the pancakes dissolved as quickly as they'd been eaten.

"Fuck!" he yelled and got up, moving jerkily, feeling suddenly incapable of moving any other way. He pulled on his pants and shirt and left the room, slamming the door on his way out.

"Hey!" He heard a shout from the room next to his. "Keep it quiet; people are trying to get laid here!" The comment was followed by a brief titter of female laughter.

Luis' sight was clouded suddenly by a dark redness, and a surge of rage rolled up from his stomach and into his brain; he found that he couldn't control himself anymore, and that he didn't really want to.

He kicked in the door.

An old man was in bed, his flabby white ass bare to the world, nestled between the legs of a much younger girl, surely no more than half his age. The air was moist with the smells of sex and body odor, and for a moment Luis was almost sick with it.

"What did you say?" he said, reaching into his pocket. "What did you say to me, you old sack of bones?" He walked into the room. He felt like his eyes were about to jump from their sockets, electrified.

"N-nothing," the old man said, standing up, his half-erect pecker swinging back and forth like an increasingly flaccid divining rod as he moved. "I didn't say nothing at all."

Luis took his hand out of his pocket, and with a flick of his wrist the straight razor opened. He could feel the fear flowing off of them both now, and it excited him even more.

"That's not quite true, now is it?" he said, advancing on the half-naked man. The girl in the bed tried to make a run for it with the sheet wrapped around her body, but Luis reached out with the razor and a long gash appeared in her arm, just above the elbow, deep enough to reveal white bone beneath. She screamed and fell to the ground, bleeding badly, pressing her free hand over the breach in her body. Luis ignored her.

"You should learn to keep your big mouth shut," he said, just a few feet from the old man now.

With disgust, he saw that the old fucker was pissing himself, a stream of yellow spattering on his feet and on the carpet.

Luis lashed out with the razor and felt it slice through the skin and muscle of the old man's chest, scraping bone with a sound like stone on stone, dull. Blood ran down in a crimson curtain and the old man fell to the floor in a pool of his own piss and blood. Luis slashed down again and again, cutting defensive fingers and arms to the white, white bone.

In the distance, he heard sirens. Luis shook his head to clear it. He must have lost track of time. Looking down he saw that the thing that had been the old man was little more now than a tattered pile of ruined flesh. How could the cops already be on their way? The girl? He looked, but she was gone.

Luis left the room and hurried to his car and climbed in. In seconds he was back on the highway, heading east, that murderous feeling still humming in his body. He only wished he'd had the time and privacy to do the old fucker right.

Chapter 8

At 5:45 the next morning, Cole knocked on Sarah's door at Haverhill House and they headed down to the dock together to catch the morning ferry to the island.

Outside, it was cold and windy and flurrying a little bit, but not really snowing. To Sarah it didn't seem like she was watching flurries falling to the ground, but rather as though she were watching as the brisk wind blew the same bunch of tolerant snowflakes around in perpetuity, refusing to let them join their frigid kindred on the earth's surface.

In anticipation of the cold and snow, Sarah had dressed in thermal underwear, gray wool pants, a heavy green sweater, and waterproof boots. She also wore a pair of black leather gloves and an orange scarf, which she'd wrapped three times around her neck, tucking the leftover into her warm, down-filled coat. In the end, the only skin left vulnerable to the elements was a three-inch strip between the top of her cheeks and the bottom of the black watchman's cap she wore pulled down over the tops of her ears and forehead.

Cole was dressed in a pair of blue jeans and a red-and-black checkered, fleece-lined coat that looked like a refugee directly from the pages of an L.L.Bean catalogue. He wore no hat or gloves, but showed no signs of being cold in the least, though his cheeks and nose were bright red two minutes after they left the crispy confines of Haverhill House.

Walking with Cole in silence down the steep hill toward

the water, Sarah let herself feel comfortable and tried to enjoy the scene unfolding in front of her.

The sun was not yet up, but there was a warm, orange glow on the horizon, as though the water itself were on fire just past the point her sight could reach. A thirty-foot boat was chugging slowly out of the marina toward open sea, and Sarah could see two heavily bundled men sitting on top of boxes in the transom, their gloved hands wrapped around steaming cups of coffee, wisping cigarettes dangling from their mouths.

Farther out, small and nearly indistinguishable from the bay in the half-light of the pre-dawn morning, Sarah could see an island, and she wondered if it was the one that housed the Davies Clinic. As if he'd read her mind, Cole pointed and said, "There it is," then smiled at her.

"Pretty," Sarah said, returning the smile, though he couldn't possibly have seen it since her mouth was hidden beneath three layers of orange wool.

Cole nodded. "From here."

They reached the dock for the ferry, which bordered the marina on the south side, and climbed aboard the fifty-foot vessel.

A short, dark-complexioned man with a beard, wearing a Red Sox cap and a denim coat, nodded at Cole as they climbed aboard. Cole said, "Manny," nodded back, then guided Sarah to the rear of the boat. They took their seats on benches that ran along the inside of the hull, then waited as perhaps twenty more people boarded.

Sarah looked at Cole, puzzled, and said, "These people aren't all going to the Clinic?" From what Cole had told her of the Clinic's recent problems, she'd expected three or four people tops, and the rest of the ferry's passengers looked more like fishermen than medical staff.

"No," he replied, "the ferry hits thirteen islands three times a day: once in the morning, once in the afternoon, and then again in the evening. When we get out to the Clinic, which is the first stop, you'll be able to see some of the other islands. Right now the coastline is blocking some, and the others are really tiny and more than five miles farther out past the Clinic."

Shortly thereafter, the man Cole had called Manny tossed the lines in the aft and stern, at which Cole laughed for some reason, and the boat's engine rumbled into noisy life.

The ferry moved forward, slowly at first, then picking up some speed. As it did, Sarah noticed a marked change in Cole's demeanor.

Where before he had looked comfortable and at ease, now his hands were clenched and he looked tight and uneasy.

"What's the matter?" she said. "Don't like the water?"

"It's no big deal. Just your typical, run-of-the-mill phobia."

"There's no such thing."

"Yeah, well."

"Sort of funny that you work on an island, considering."

"Right," he said, "a real laugh riot."

A few minutes later, something occurred to Sarah. Turning to Cole, she said, "Where's Doctor Davies? He doesn't live out there, does he?"

Cole looked surprised. "I thought I told you over the phone. He's got pneumonia. Bad. For at least the next two or three days, he's the property of Saint Joseph's Memorial Hospital in Portland. Probably longer than that."

"So who looks after the girl at night?"

"After the last RN disappeared, I hired another temporary replacement from the agency in Freeport."

Sarah looked puzzled. "Why don't you just move her off the island?"

"That would be great," Cole said. "Believe me, I'd love to, but there's no other place for her."

"But there has to be somewhere, maybe in Portland or Boston? New York, for Christ's sake!"

Shaking his head, Cole said, "Davies would never agree to that. Never."

"Why not?" The more Sarah thought about it, the more and more absurd it seemed. Why keep an unconscious young girl secluded on an island in the middle of nowhere, when she could be getting comparable, or even superior, attention elsewhere?

"I know it's difficult to understand," Cole said, "but you have to look at it from his point of view. This is his granddaughter we're talking about, his only remaining family, and she's in a coma. And this is his clinic, his life, which is dedicated to helping people in exactly her situation. If she leaves, then it's over, everything he's worked for."

Sarah took a deep breath and then blew it derisively out through her nose. "I don't know, Cole. That sounds like pretty selfish reasoning to me. And dangerous for the girl, too. I mean, look. She's out here, with two miles of water between her and . . . anything, all night, with only a temp to take care of her? That's the worst kind of irresponsible. What if something goes wrong? What if there's a fire? Or a flood? He's playing with her life."

"No! No, he's not!" Cole stood up and grasped the rail, the color in his face now the result of more than the frigid air. "He's not playing games with her life, Sarah. He's trying to save it. He feels like this is the only place Cora's going to get what she needs to pull through this thing. And I think he's right. He can help her. I can help her. I can feel that."

Sarah looked up and scrutinized him, searching his eyes for any sign of uncertainty, but saw none. Whatever his feelings were, and wherever they came from, they were based on more than just a hunch; it was more like conviction, absolute and unquestionable. All right, she thought, just let it go. We'll see how today goes, and if I think something more needs to be said tonight, I'll cross that bridge then.

Wanting to smooth things over, she smiled at Cole, squinting a little into the just barely visible sun, and saw him relax visibly.

"So," she said, trying for a jocular tone, "you can feel it? What, are you psychic now, too?" He looked down at her for a moment longer, before chuckling and retaking his seat.

"Sorry," he said, "I didn't mean to go off like that."

"No sweat," Sarah said, "it just means you care."

As they began their approach to the island about fifteen minutes later, an unsettling feeling crept over Sarah and she found herself unable to remain seated.

She stood up and walked, first to the front of the fifty-foot craft, then to the back, and then back to the midsection of the boat, where Cole sat.

Up ahead the island bobbed amidst the whitecaps, perhaps a mile long and half as wide. Sarah could see a slash of white perched atop the sole hill of the island, and she assumed it was the Clinic.

"Something the matter?" Cole said, half-rising, seeing her uneasiness. "Are you going to be sick or—"

She waved him off. "No, it's not that, it's just—Jesus, Cole, can't you feel it?" The air was sharp, buzzing with energy. She could actually hear it, like a swarm of angry wasps, and getting stronger the closer they came to the island.

Sarah put her hands over her ears, but it did nothing to quell the sound. She felt a prickling along her arms and legs and at the back of her neck, and became aware suddenly that she could feel everything. The rubbing of her pants against her legs was unbearable. The cold air sliced through her heavy clothing and slashed at her suddenly hypersensitive skin like a razor. Panic began to set in.

"Come on, Sarah," she whispered, grabbing the rail and gripping it tightly with both hands, "get control."

She envisioned herself, just as she was now, standing on the ferry, holding onto the rail, brown hair blowing in the stiff wind. The powerful energy that was threatening to usurp her self-control was blue in the air. It crackled and sparkled like the tiny phosphorescent animals in the deep ocean sparkle at night. In her mind, she too was alight with the blue energy, but now Sarah took a deep breath, filling her lungs with as much air as she could take in, then breathed it out, expelling with it a cloud of shimmering blue. She repeated the process, then again, and again, until she was empty of everything except herself and oxygen. Now she envisioned a green sphere surrounding her, green because it was a safe color to her, a protective one, holding the shimmering blueness at bay. It would protect her for now, but how long would it last?

She opened her eyes and was not surprised to see that the island was now near, but she felt in control again and sat back down with Cole, feeling suddenly tired but anxious, a discomfiting contradiction in mental states.

"Everything okay?" he said, eyeing her cautiously, as though she might erupt at any moment in a volcano of throw-up.

"Fine now."

The ferry docked. Cole and Sarah climbed off and headed up the path toward the Clinic, accompanied only by a brown-haired girl Cole greeted as Dana.

"What happened back there on the boat?" Cole said as

they made their way up the path. "And don't tell me it was nothing, because I don't buy it."

"I felt something," she answered tersely, "that's all." Her head was pounding from the effort it took to keep her mental shield up, and Cole's questions were distracting.

"What kind of something?"

"Cole," she said, stopping and turning toward him, about to snap and hating herself for it, "I . . ." Over his shoulder, something caught her eye and whatever she had been about to say died in her throat.

An enormous bridge, wide and tall, struck off from the edge of the island near the dock and into the ocean, where it was engulfed at the midway point by an opaque white mist. The girders were blue and bright, and heavy wire cable stretched from the ground up a hundred feet to a pointed apex and then back down again, in a series of gently sloping parabolas. Four lanes of clean asphalt stretched out into the mist, lined brightly in white and yellow. It looked like a smaller version of the Golden Gate, but in blue, not coppery red.

"Oh my God," she whispered, "there's . . ." But suddenly it was gone, vanished, leaving Sarah to wonder if she'd even seen it at all.

"What?" Cole said. "What is it?"

She shook her head, trying to clear it, and forced a smile. "I'm sorry. I guess I'm just still a little tired. Long trip up from Philly, you know. Driving kills my eyes." Inside her head, she could feel the fatigue growing. Had she really seen the bridge, or had the strange image just been the result of her weariness, a maverick intruder from some previous thought? Unable to spare the energy it took to sort out the possible explanations, she shooed the matter from her conscious mind and determined to deal with it later.

"Right," Cole said, but she saw in his eyes that he didn't believe her.

They went straight to Cora's room.

Cole closed the door and checked the chart at the foot of the girl's bed. Sarah looked around at the surroundings, feeling faint now. She leaned against the wall and closed her eyes, trying to gather strength. The power in the air was amazing; she'd never experienced anything remotely like it. It was like standing inside a room where a nuclear reaction was building.

For the first time, Sarah admitted to herself that she was absolutely terrified.

She looked at the bed where Cora lay so still, only her chest moving, slowly, up and down. Horrified, Sarah realized that the girl's skin was glowing blue, and that when she exhaled, it was visible, a thousand little crystals of blue hanging in the air above her mouth for the briefest of moments before dissipating.

"Cole," she said, only a faint whisper coming out, "get me out of here. Please, right now. Please." It was hard to breathe; she was overwhelmed. The air suddenly smelled like cherry blossoms. It was hot, incredibly hot, and she couldn't breathe, couldn't breathe. She was aware of her legs giving away, and then all was black.

Chapter 9

Cole was lying on the couch in his living room, watching TV and resisting the urge to doze, when Sarah opened the door and came out of the bedroom. She looked tired, but better than she had earlier. Her face was no longer as pale as it had been, and the dark, bruised-looking areas beneath both of her eyes were less pronounced.

Seeing her like this, fresh from sleep, and from his bed, Cole couldn't help but think of how little she had really changed since Duke. Still passionate, still strong, and still heartbreakingly beautiful. Not for the first time, he wondered how different his life might have been if he'd held onto her all those years ago, if he'd been different from everyone else in her life and stayed there for her when she really needed him. The line of thought threatened to engulf him, and he shoved it quickly away. No use baiting himself with the past.

"What time is it?" she said, running her hands through her hair, which was sprouting out in a thousand directions. She was still dressed in the wool pants and sweater she'd worn to the Clinic that morning, and they were as rumpled as the rest of her.

"Sevenish."

"I was out for an hour!" she exclaimed.

"No," Cole said, shaking his head and grinning, "seven p.m. You were asleep all day. I managed to get us back on the ferry before it returned to the mainland this morning. You've been asleep ever since."

She gawked, unbelieving, and Cole couldn't help but laugh at her reaction. Sarah walked to the big easy chair by the fireplace, sat down, and leaned back into it, letting the soft cushions swallow her up.

"Want a beer?" Cole said, standing. Sarah nodded, apparently not yet capable of speech. He had the feeling that if he'd offered a live rattlesnake, she would have nodded at that, too.

He went to the kitchen and returned with two Coronas and handed one to Sarah. She raised it to her mouth and sipped eagerly, and then again, until half the beer was gone, then sat back again and stared into the fire. Cole looked at her and waited for her to say something, but she didn't, just drank her beer. When she finished it, Cole asked her if she wanted another, and she nodded. He returned with it and sat back down.

Finally, she spoke.

"What do you know about psychics, Cole? I'm using the term 'psychic' loosely here, just a rainbow definition for people with supernormal mental capabilities."

"Not much, really. Just what I've seen in the movies and what you told me when I was a twenty-five-year-old bonehead med student." Cole grinned sheepishly. "Mind-reading, prognostication, telekinesis. That kind of stuff."

Sarah scoffed. "Pigeonholing psychics that way is just a polite way of saying they don't exist, that it's all some kind of cheesy hoax. Much more fun to laugh at a telekinete or a pyrokinete than just a plain old psychic."

"Well, excuse me for being born."

Smiling ruefully, she said, "Sorry. Hazard of the condition, overprotectiveness of your own and all that. We don't exactly get a lot of good press, you know. What I was trying to get at," Sarah said, taking another deep swig of her beer, "is that there are basically two kinds of psychics, receivers and transmitters. I've never seen anyone who can do both. Until today, until I walked into that girl's room and found myself on the edge of—Jesus, I don't even know what. I felt as though I was on the verge of being . . . enveloped by her. I felt my individuality being sucked away, and it was all I could do to stop it from happening. I have to tell you, Cole, that was the scariest thing that's ever happened to me. I went in there with my defenses up, and I still lost it. And it only took a few seconds." Sarah found that she was shaking, remembering the events of the morning. "And the most terrifying thing is that I don't think that what I felt this morning is anything more than the palest shadow of her full strength."

"You think she's dangerous?" Cole said, eyes wide in surprise. "But she's just a kid, a comatose little girl."

"Come on, Cole!" Sarah said. "Isn't that why you called me in the first place, because you thought Cora had something to do with that RN disappearing?" Sarah was rankled now. She hated the closed-mindedness of even the most liberal of people, people who thought they could accept the truth, but who, in the end, were just as unwilling to make that vital leap as everyone else.

"Yeah, sure, but—"

"But nothing!" Sarah said. "If you're not going to listen to what I have to say, then why'd you ask me to come here in the first place?"

Cole started to respond, then stopped. She was right, he knew she was. He didn't know why he was being so stubborn about this. He'd had his suspicions even before Sarah arrived.

"Look," Cole said, "I apologize. You're right. I do believe

you. This is just unfamiliar ground for me." There was a silence, and then he said, "Is there anything we can do, Sarah? I mean, can you help her?"

Sarah stood up. "I need to think about that, Cole. I need to give that some very serious thought." Walking to the kitchen counter and setting her empty beer bottle on the white Formica surface, she said, "In the meantime, I'm famished."

She showered and, when she was out and dressed, he took her for pizza at Vic's, his favorite place in town.

Cole was halfway though his second piece of mushroom and pineapple pizza, when he looked across the table at Sarah and found her staring out at the gray waters of the bay.

"Everything okay, Sarah?" he said.

She looked at him and smiled faintly. "Even here, this far away, I can feel her, tugging at my mind."

"What do you mean?"

"Psychics are essentially like magnets, some charged one way, some charged the other way, pushing and pulling each other," Sarah said. "I pass people on the street all the time who possess varying levels of psychic ability—"

At this, Cole looked at her, a quizzical look on his face. Sarah laughed lightheartedly and said, "That's right, there are more of us out there than you can know, even than I can know. Not that everyone has the same level of ability, and most don't ever realize their gift. The overwhelming majority of people just don't possess the imagination to be able to conceptualize the forces at work when they . . . well, for example, when they get a feeling that any minute Aunt Edna is going to call on the phone, and then she does. Or when they know the moment they wake up that today is the day they'll hear from a friend they haven't spoken to in twenty years. Those things aren't just coincidence or dumb luck. They happen for a reason, but very few people ever learn to harness those latent abilities, or even see them for what they are."

"But you did," Cole said.

Sarah looked at him contemplatively for a few moments. "It look a lot of work, and a lot of heartache, before I was able to accept my gift. I lost most of the people I cared about, before I was able to work through the issues I needed to resolve. I'm only just beginning to get some of those people back. My old friends, my parents—" She looked up at Cole, and it was all he could do not to drop his gaze to the table in shame.

They sat in complete silence for almost a minute, before Sarah spoke again.

"I don't blame you for leaving, Cole."

"You don't have to," he said softly, "I blame myself enough for both of us. I was a selfish asshole."

She shook her head. "You were young. We both were. If I were in your shoes, I'd likely have done the same thing."

Cole's hands were resting folded on the table in front of him, and now Sarah put one of her own over them.

"After all," she said, "it's not every day your live-in girlfriend starts reciting your thoughts for you before you even know you're having them, breaking into fits of depression every time another woman walks by because she knows exactly what you're thinking, revealing your deepest, darkest secrets to you, even the ones you didn't know you had, holding them over you . . . I was young, too, Cole. Young, and drunk with a new power I couldn't control. I don't blame you. Even then I didn't; I just wasn't secure enough to tell you that."

He looked her in the eyes, a pained expression on his face. "Do you really mean that, or are you just saying it to make me feel like less of a prick?"

"I'm not just saying it."

He placed one of his big hands over one of her small ones. They sat in comfortable silence for a few moments, before a thought suddenly occurred to Cole.

"Did you ever feel any psychic pull from me?" he said, smiling a little bit at the thought of himself in possession of psychic abilities.

"No," she said, "the attraction I felt from you was a different kind altogether. When you encounter a psychic, it's like you've walked past the entrance to a wind tunnel. The energy they create can be positive or negative, and it either pulls you in or repels you. Most people's wind tunnels aren't very powerful, though, no more than a slight breeze. If you find someone who has also managed to harness their abilities, sometimes it feels more like a strong gust, but still, nothing dangerous." Her features darkened suddenly. "With Cora, though, it's like . . . it's like trying to resist the pull of a psychic black hole. The only safe thing is to stay far enough away that she can't influence you. But even from here I can feel her mind sucking at mine, trying to draw it in. I've never felt anything quite like it. This is going to sound grossly egotistical, but I've never met a psychic more powerful than me. Until now."

Sarah leaned her elbows on the table and rested her chin tiredly on top of her joined palms, realizing suddenly how beat she still felt. "If my abilities are like a pair of paper cups connected by a length of string," she said, "then hers are a nuclear-powered HAM radio, and that's a conservative comparison. It's remarkable."

She looked down at the table. "I think I can help her, Cole. I want to try."

Chapter 10

The black car roared down the empty highway, eating up the road with tires that left tracks of orange fire in their wake.

Always before, Luis had been suspended above and behind the car, only an observer, but not now. Now he was the driver, looking out at the empty world from behind the windshield, pushing his foot down on the gas pedal until it clicked on the floor, hands gripping the steering wheel so tightly that the leather creaked.

He wasn't being taken anymore; he was going.

Signs whipped by on his left, signs for places he'd never been in his life: Blue Springs, Terre Haute, Columbus, Valley Forge, Hartford. East, east, east. He was going to where he was supposed to be.

And now, far up ahead, there was a light: tiny, like a pinprick in a piece of thick black velvet draped over an incandescent light bulb. It was still far off, but he was getting closer.

Always closer.

Chapter 11

The next morning, when they arrived at the Clinic, Cole informed Dana that for most of the day he and Sarah would be working with Cora, and that they were not to be interrupted. The young RN looked somewhat puzzled, but said that if she was needed, she'd be in the duty-office, reviewing files. Cole knew that since there were no files to review, that likely meant she would be drinking coffee and doing crossword puzzles.

Their privacy ensured, Cole and Sarah headed down to Cora's room.

A preternatural silence filled the Clinic, a quiet so thick and stifling that Sarah felt she could have screamed at the top of her lungs and not made a dent in the hanging pall of noiselessness. Even their footsteps sounded dull and far off. And it wasn't just the sound. Somehow, the color seemed to have bled out of everything: the floors, the walls, even her own clothing. Colors were drab imitations of their former selves. Even black and white seemed to have run into each other, creating an unremarkable gray. She wondered if the dullness of her senses was shared by Cole, or if she alone was experiencing the effects of Cora's psychic vortex.

As Cole and Sarah were making their way down the hall toward Cora's room, Sarah's knees suddenly felt weak. She stumbled and almost fell, but Cole caught her.

"Are you okay?" he said, holding her tightly around the waist.

"Just get me there fast," she said, her face strained, "really fast. I'm losing it again."

"Right." Cole put her arm around his shoulders. He could feel her slim body shaking, and the skin of her arm was hot on his neck. He couldn't see if her eyes were open, but her breathing was hitchy and labored, as though she'd just finished running a marathon.

He helped her down the hall and unlocked the door to Cora's room, then guided her inside.

Cole leaned Sarah against the wall and slid a folding chair over from the window to the bed. He ushered Sarah over to the chair and eased her down into it, holding her gently by the shoulders. She slumped over, massaging her temples with the tips of her fingers as though she was holding her skull together with the pressure.

"How long is this going to take?" he said.

"Don't know," she murmured, her voice so faint that Cole could hardly hear it. "I've only done this once before, and that person wasn't psychic. I have no idea what's going to happen."

It felt for all the world like some determined lunatic was trying to beat their way into her skull with a dull-edged pickaxe, and goddamn if she wasn't just about to drop her guard, willingly, and let them take their best shot. It was crazy, what she was about to do. Jesus, what the hell was she thinking?

With considerable effort, Sarah sat up and took her hands from her head, trying with every ounce of strength she possessed to keep herself together. She took a deep breath, then another, clearing her mind of all extraneous thoughts, creating, as best she could, a *tabula rasa*, a white screen on the surface of her mind, ready to receive whatever input Cora threw her way. Exhaling her last breath and opening her eyes, she said, "Here goes nothing."

Cora was lying with her hands at her sides. Sarah reached out and took one of them in her own, feeling a bizarre anticipatory terror building inside her. *This is insane,* she thought, *I have no idea what this is going to do to me. Or to her.*

She let her eyes shut again, and then, trying to disregard the fear twisting in the pit of her stomach, dropped her wall, opening herself to the girl's powerful mind.

There was a split-second feeling of being sucked forward and then of stopping short, her body remaining in place while the rest of her continued ahead for another few feet before snapping back to rejoin her, like mental whiplash. It left her feeling vaguely nauseated, not as if she were going to vomit, but as if she were drunk with the spins.

When the dizziness passed, she found herself lying flat on her back, the floor of the Clinic hard beneath her, even through her sweater.

It hadn't worked; nothing had happened. *Damn,* she thought, *what went wrong?*

She opened her eyes.

Darkness. But not complete darkness. Above, there were sprinkles of light in the sky. Stars?

From somewhere nearby, a repeated sound. Dripping. Water dripping into water. Plonk. Plonk. Plonk. Regular as clockwork. She realized that she was warm, almost hot.

This wasn't the Clinic.

Sarah bolted into sitting position, panic buzzing through her brain. Where was she? And, more important, how had she gotten here?

She stood slowly, still spinning a bit, and looked around her. Her eyes were slowly adapting to the relative darkness and she realized that she was on a street, a gently sloping street bordered on both sides by tall, bushy trees and hedges, a street along which nobody walked or drove.

She was alone. Completely alone.

"What is this?" she said, hands clenching tightly into fists, terrified but trying to keep herself together. This all had to be explainable somehow. The last thing she remembered was being with Cole in Cora's room, feeling the girl's mind pounding away at hers, demanding surrender, demanding access. Had something happened there, something bad? The thought flashed through her mind that she could be suffering from some sort of amnesia, that the goings-on at the Clinic might have taken place months, or even years, ago. What if this was where she lived now? Would she be able to find her way home? Or what if there had never been any Clinic at all? No girl, no island. No Cole. God, what was happening to her?

All right, she thought, *control yourself. You're not insane, but if you don't get a grip right now, you will be soon.*

She turned and looked behind her, her eyes much more accustomed to the dearth of light now.

There was a tall bridge in the distance, a bridge she recognized, with blue girders and sloping parabolas of thick cable coming to points high above the lanes of asphalt. After a hundred feet or so, the bridge was engulfed by a thick mist and Sarah couldn't see to the other side.

The bridge from the island, she thought. That's the bridge I saw my first day at the Clinic. Choosing to disregard the very unlikely possibility that she'd actually been teleported away from the island, Sarah could only see two possible explanations for her current situation. Either she was being manifested physically inside her own mind, or she was inside Cora's.

She turned back around.

In front of and below her was a town, one she most certainly did not recognize. The streets she could see were lined with trees and light poles. Oddly, though, none of the lights were on.

After a moment's thought, Sarah headed down the gentle decline toward the town, noticing, as she did, that there was a pleasant smell in the warm air of cherry blossoms.

At the foot of the hill, in a circular, grassy plot at the middle of an old-fashioned traffic circle, there was a fountain mounted atop a pedestal which rose from the center of a round, three-foot high, marble basin.

The fountain was in the shape of a sailing-ship, an old cutter, sails at full mast. Water flowed in clear streams from the mouths of four canons that sprouted from both sides of the ship's hull.

Sarah saw that a bronze plaque was mounted on a podium facing back toward the hill she had just walked down. WELCOME TO BRIDGEWATER, A TOWN OF PEACE AND GOOD WILL, it read. ESTABLISHED 1876. More had been written underneath that, but the words were smudgy and too faint for Sarah to read in the dim light.

What? Bridgewater? Where in the name of God was Bridgewater?

A scuffing noise startled her and she nearly screamed. Her eyes moved frantically from the plaque to the street, but all she saw was the dark town in front of her.

Taking a deep breath, she moved around the fountain, keeping her hands on the reassuringly cool stone of the basin. She felt watched, could feel the hairs on the back of her neck standing stiffly at attention.

In front of her, the street stretched out into what looked like the commercial sector of the town.

Immediately to her right, a large, house-like building proclaimed itself City Hall by way of a white banner with black lettering stretched between two windows on the third floor.

Past that, the street was lined with trees on the left, and shops on the right. Beyond the trees, Sarah could see a slide and a merry-go-round. A playground.

She started forward, feeling now as though a thousand pairs of eyes were trained on her, her skin crawling with their touches.

There was motion ahead, near the trees. Sarah froze.

Whatever it was, she could almost see it now, skulking in the shadows. A dog, maybe. Maybe not. Either way, she wasn't helping herself by standing around. Better that she keep moving. If it hadn't attacked her yet, maybe that meant it wasn't interested.

By the time she reached the first of the shops, the thing in the shadows wasn't trying to be quiet anymore.

It tromped over twigs and dead leaves, making loud snapping and popping noises. Several times it moved from one shadow to another and Sarah caught fleeting glimpses of it, something small, but ungodly fast.

She tried the door to the first of the shops, a small store with a sign reading: SPRINGER'S ICE CREAM in the large plate-glass window, and found that it was locked. Oh man, she thought, what are they going to put as cause of death in my death certificate if I end up a late dinner for an imaginary dog?

She moved on down the sidewalk past darkened London-style street lamps and decorative saplings planted at intervals in plots near the sidewalk's curb, trying the doors to shop after shop, finding none of them open. And then something occurred to her. She wasn't actually here. Her body was back in the Clinic, sitting in a chair beside Cora's bed. Whatever happened to her in this imaginary town was no more real than the things that occurred in her dreams, only these dreams weren't hers, they were someone else's. Someone else's very realistic dreams, but dreams nonetheless.

Sarah turned toward the street, trying to banish from her mind the fear she was still feeling. On the other side, the thing moved in the darkness beneath the trees. *Not a dog,* she thought, *too tall. It's a person.*

Stepping forward off the sidewalk and into the street, Sarah said, "Who are you?" She tried to keep her voice steady and thought she did a good job, considering.

There was no response.

Sarah stopped halfway across the street, listening. The silence was complete.

Sucking in another breath, Sarah said, louder this time, "I want to see Cora."

The thing exploded toward her out of the darkness and Sarah squawked, back-pedaling frantically, hands up in front of her face.

Her heels hit the curb of the sidewalk and she fell awkwardly on her butt, sending a nasty jolt up her spine. She curled into a ball with her hand over her face and screamed, waiting for the thing to attack her.

But no teeth ripped into her flesh, no animal growl deafened her ears. Sarah opened her eyes and peered out from behind her sheltering arms . . . and saw Cora.

The girl was dressed in black pants and a black T-shirt. Her hair was tied back in a ponytail, fully revealing her pretty face, streaked and smudged with dirt.

"Never say my name here," she said, crouching beside Sarah, looking back over each shoulder, eyes scanning the empty street fearfully. "Never."

Getting some of her breath back, Sarah said, "Why not?"

"Come on, we have to go." Cora reached out a hand and helped Sarah to her feet. Sarah was surprised at how real she felt and, for that matter, how real the pain in her ass and both of her hands felt.

She turned her palms up and looked at them. Both were scored with bloody cuts from the loose gravel on the sidewalk. Plucking a piece of rock from underneath a flap of skin, she hissed in pain. "This really hurts," she said, looking wide-eyed at Cora.

"Come on." Cora started off down the street, back the way Sarah had just come. Sarah followed, breaking into a slow jog to keep up with the fleet-footed girl.

"Hey," she said, puffing a little from the exertion, "where are we going?"

Cora didn't answer, just kept on moving. They reached the row of stores and swung left across what Sarah thought must be the town park, a narrow, grassy stretch filled with trees and benches. Ahead there was a big brick building. The high school.

"What's going on here, Cora?" Sarah said, fighting to keep up with her. Cora stopped short and Sarah nearly rammed into her back.

"I told you not to call me that!" Cora said through clenched teeth. "Do you want to get us both killed?"

"Why can't I say your name?"

Cora started to respond, then saw something over Sarah's shoulder and sucked in a breath. "Oh, shit," she said, "he's here. Come on, quick."

Sarah turned to look for what the girl was talking about. Just before she was yanked bodily forward by the arm, she thought she saw a large shape coming toward them through the park, moving fast.

Cora sprinted toward the school, dragging Sarah along by the hand. They crossed a parking lot, completely empty of cars, then hopped up the curb and through a break in the fence onto the athletic fields.

Sarah's lungs were burning; she was fighting to keep her

legs moving and didn't know how much longer she could keep up the pace. Suddenly, at the edge of the wide field, Cora yanked her to the left and pulled her into the shadows underneath a set of gray, metallic bleachers. Through the spaces between levels of benches, Sarah could see the dark shape coming quickly, carried by long legs. It passed through the break in the fence and headed their way. In another twenty seconds it would be upon them.

"What is it?" Sarah asked, heaving for breath, her heart pounding inside her rib cage. "Why did we stop?"

Cora turned to Sarah and held out her hands, palms up. Unquestioning, Sarah took them. She could feel the young girl's hands shaking as badly as her own.

"Now close your eyes," Cora said, and Sarah did.

There was that feeling again of being sucked forward, and then the jolting stop.

Sarah opened her eyes.

Chapter 12

Bright sunlight slanted through the spaces between the bleachers' levels and into Sarah's eyes like golden knives, blinding her.

She shielded her eyes with her hands and looked around, trying to get her bearings. From all around there were voices, loud and excited, cheering. Also the smells of cigarette smoke and freshly mowed grass. A gentle, warm breeze passed over her face.

"Come on," she heard Cora say urgently, "we don't have much time. It never takes him long to find the way in." A hand gripped her high up on the arm and she let herself be led out from underneath the bleachers, sliding her feet along, trying not to trip over anything. After a few seconds, her eyes adjusted enough to the light that she could look where she was going.

They were moving through a crowd, Cora in the lead, angling around young people in shorts and t-shirts, and older people, parents, wearing dresses and shirts and ties.

On the field she and Cora had just run across, a girl's soccer game was in progress, one of the teams sporting red and yellow uniforms, the other blue and black. Cora was wearing one of the blue and black ones. BRIDGEWATER GATORS was printed across the back of her jersey, along with the number 13. Her long, brown hair was tied back with a black scrunchie and swished back and forth across her back as she moved.

They broke from the crowd and ran toward the high school across a series of concrete basketball courts. Cora had on soccer cleats and her feet clacked hollowly on the paved surface as she led them through an open door and into the school, passing a pair of kids who stared at them as they passed.

"Lookin' good, Cora," one of the kids, a blond boy about Cora's own age, called after them. She ignored him and headed up the stairs, taking them three at a time, dragging Sarah behind her, then slammed through the double doors leading to the next floor.

"Where are you going?" Sarah puffed, now really about to fall down. Her legs felt like Jell-O and her lungs were on fire.

Cora suddenly slammed on the brakes in front of a bank of lockers, skidding on her cleats along the waxed floor of the hallway. She grabbed the combination lock on the locker-door and dialed three numbers in quickly, then pulled the door open and rummaged through the seemingly random mess of loose papers inside.

"Eureka," she said and pulled forth a bunch of keys on a chain adorned with about a hundred charms and rings and other dangling decorations.

"What are those for?" Sarah said.

"The car."

They made it back to the parking lot in twenty seconds and Cora guided them to a black BMW parked near the basketball courts they had crossed to reach the school.

"Uh-oh," Cora said, as she was unlocking her door, "here he comes again."

Sarah looked back toward the field where the soccer game was still taking place and saw a man dressed in black coming around the edge of the bleachers, headed their way. She couldn't make out his face from so far away, but noticed that there was something . . . off . . . about the way the man looked.

Tearing her gaze away from him, she opened her door and fell into the car, felt the engine purr into life as Cora turned the key in the ignition and put the car into drive, then slammed her foot down on the accelerator and peeled out.

She took the turn out of the parking lot at fifty miles an hour and was going seventy a few seconds after that.

"Who was that?" Sarah asked, looking over at Cora, whose eyes were fixed on the road before her.

"The man who murdered my family." She said the words with no emotion, matter-of-factly.

Not sure she'd heard what she thought she had, Sarah said, "That's impossible; this is all inside your mind. That can't possibly be him."

Glancing over at her, Cora said, "Do you want to go back and ask him about it? Hold on." Going eighty, they flew by a Methodist church with a tall steeple, then slowed down just enough to avoid flipping as Cora swung the car left onto a narrow side street.

"Dammit," Sarah heard the girl whisper, a note of frustration evident in her voice, "this street isn't supposed to be here." She jerked the wheel to the left and the Beemer went sideways through an intersection, gained traction, then peeled ahead again.

"What's wrong?" Sarah said, hands clamped onto the door handle so hard her knuckles were white.

"The roads are all messed up," Cora said, then suddenly saw something and slammed her foot down on the brake, throwing them both forward against the dash. She spun the steering wheel left and guided the car onto a narrow street lined with tall oak trees.

Cora pulled the car to a stop in front of a big white colonial and jumped out. "Inside," she said. "Hurry."

Cora led her through the front door and up a wide flight of stairs, then down a long hall to a bedroom, closing the door as they stepped inside.

On the walls were posters of soccer and field hockey players. The bed was covered with a white quilt embroidered with basketballs and soccer balls. Sarah walked over to the small desk which occupied one corner and picked up a pink frame in the shape of a heart. In it was a picture of Cora with an older man and woman and a young boy. Her parents and brother, Sarah realized. This was Cora's house, Cora's bedroom.

Sarah turned, still holding the framed picture, and found Cora sitting on the bed, staring at her.

"That man," Sarah said. "You run from him all the time?"

"Yes," Cora said, "but it's getting harder and harder to stay ahead of him. It used to be easy, but he's getting faster, smarter."

"What did you mean when you said he was the man who murdered your family? How is that possible? This isn't real; it's inside your mind."

In the familiar surroundings of her own bedroom, the girl seemed more willing to talk. Where before she had looked mature beyond her years, hardened even, now she seemed much younger than sixteen, and scared.

In a shaky voice, she began to talk, looking at the ground. "When he was . . . when he was killing my mom and dad and my little brother in the parking garage, I felt him in my mind, hateful, like he wasn't even a person at all." She shuddered at the remembered experience. "He was so powerful that it felt like he was cutting me even though he never touched me. When I ran and he chased me, I could feel how badly he wanted to do the same thing to me as he did to them, how much he wanted to cut me and to know that I was hurting, and it made him so happy to think about that. I think he wanted to know I was hurting, because that's the only way he could feel anything. Even later, when he was gone and the police came, I could still feel him out there, and inside of me. Part of him never left. It's like he wanted to kill me so badly that he left a part of himself to do the job he couldn't. The darkest part. He hunts me all the time, always just a step behind me. I don't know how much longer I can stay ahead of him." The terror in the girl's voice was unmistakable.

"Where are we now?" Sarah asked softly. "What is all this?"

"A memory," Cora answered, "a good memory. We won the league championship today."

"Today? When is this?"

Cora stood up and walked over to a dark, wooden bookshelf. She picked up a plastic trophy with a girl kicking a soccer ball mounted on the top and handed it to Sarah. A gold plastic plaque on the base said: BRIDGEWATER HIGH SCHOOL INTER-AC CHAMPS 1997.

"That's two years ago," Sarah said.

Cora nodded. "My sophomore year." Cora locked Sarah's eyes with her own. "You have to leave here now."

Sarah nodded and smiled. "We both do. You have to come with me, Co—"

"No, don't!" Cora yelled and grabbed Sarah by the shoulders. "Don't say it!"

"Why? Why can't I say your name?"

"Because as long as I want to stay alive, I can't be her. I can't be me. If I even think about that, he knows and he comes for me. I have to lay low, in the shadows, try to be no one."

"Then we'll leave," Sarah said. "We'll both get out of this place. Right now."

"No," she said, "I can't leave. I've tried a hundred times, but I can't get out."

"There has to be a way. If there's a way in, there's a way out. That's just common sense."

Cora nodded. "I know. I spend all my time looking. I'll find it. I just hope I find it soon." She paused. "Something's changing."

"Then I should stay and help you look," Sarah said. "Four eyes are better than two."

Cora shook her head. "You'd only slow me down. This is my turf. That's the only reason I've been able to stay alive this long. I need to do this by myself."

Going against every instinct in her body, Sarah said, "Maybe you're right." She felt horrible at the prospect of leaving Cora here by herself to deal with all of this, but it seemed the only real option.

"I know I am," Cora said, holding out her hands, which Sarah took in her own. "You know the drill."

Sarah closed her eyes and when she opened them, Cora was once again dressed in black, face dirty and dark. The nameless shadow.

When they went downstairs and out the door, Sarah was not surprised to see that the car was gone, and that it was once again night, lightless night.

Sarah was beginning to feel strange, lightheaded and tired. A pain, somehow faraway and portentous, like the first signs of a really bad migraine, began throbbing in her head, just behind her eyes.

"What's happening?" she said, her words badly slurred.

"You have to go," she heard Cora say from somewhere far away, and then Sarah stumbled and fell hard to the ground, hitting her chin. Blue and red flowers blossomed in front of her eyes.

She groaned and tried to sit up, and from galaxies away heard a voice telling her to stay still, don't try to move. A face swam gradually into fuzzy focus far above her, and she had time to realize that it was Cole's, not Cora's, before she passed out.

Chapter 13

Luis took the Portsmouth, New Hampshire exit off I-95 and pulled into the parking lot of the first hotel he saw, a Holiday Inn with an adjoining pool and workout center.

The clock on the Mustang's dash read 3:13 a.m., which meant he'd been driving for seventeen hours, since St. Louis, without a break, except to get gas and relieve himself. He'd never been so exhausted in his life, and the pain in his head had returned with a vengeance.

Once inside, Luis walked over the counter and waited while the clerk, a young girl, certainly no older than eighteen, talked on the phone, apparently with her boyfriend.

"So you'll be here?" she said, turning away from Luis with an irritated glance, as if he were inconveniencing her, as if he were invading her goddamned privacy. She whispered a few more words into the phone, smiling like an imbecile, and then hung up and turned to Luis, the smile fading from her fat, pasty face in half a second.

"Yeah?" the girl said, looking at him down her crooked nose, like she was the Queen of Portsmouth-fucking-New Hampshire. Luis wondered through the pulsing pain in his brain if her nose had been broken. He wondered if the boy on the other end of the line had done it to her. He wondered if she'd liked it.

"I need a room for—"

The phone rang.

"Just a second," the girl said and held up a hand, reaching for the phone with the other, Luis forgotten already.

"Don't touch that phone," Luis said quietly. "Don't you dare touch that phone."

The girl must have seen something in the look on his face, because she pulled back her hand, letting the phone ring, and smiled uneasily at him. "Just one night?" she said.

He prepaid for the room with a credit card and the girl handed him a key. Turning away from the girl, Luis said, "You made the right choice. I'd have had your fat little guts for garters."

His head was on fire. The pain had gotten even worse the last few hours, since about the time he crossed the New York border, and, combined with the fatigue which was finally beginning to take its toll, it was just too much. He couldn't go any farther tonight.

Luis took the elevator to the second floor of the hotel, found his room, and inserted the key-card. The lock snapped open. He stumbled inside and barely made it to the bed before collapsing.

And still he couldn't sleep.

For an hour he lay on the bed, not moving, his mind in fast-forward.

On the road for two days without a break, he'd found himself with nothing to do but think, and the only thing he'd concluded was that he was scared. More so than he'd ever been in his life. The murderous feelings wouldn't turn off the way they usually did, the way they always did. He wanted to kill everyone he passed or saw: the people on the streets, in their cars, everyone. Wanted to cut their stomachs open with his razor and sink his teeth into their purple guts, to taste their blood on his lips. Only through their pain could he feel complete; it was the only thing that would fill the burning emptiness inside of him, even if just for a while.

With feverish vividness, he recalled the face of the girl at the check-in desk. She'd be a joy to slice and—

No, goddammit! He rolled over and buried his head in a pillow. Killing that fat sow wasn't going to help a thing! The only thing which would was taking care of the girl from his visions. Of that he was increasingly certain. Why else would he have been drawn this far?

Just thirty-some hours ago he'd woken in his own bed in L.A. and headed to work, and now he was in New Hampshire. New Hampshire! Thousands of miles from home. And whatever was pulling him along didn't seem to be anywhere near done yet, not by a long stretch. The nagging thought Luis' mind kept returning to was the chance that Crothers would stop by to check up on him, nosy bastard that he was, find that there was no answer at the door, and bust his way in, thinking that Luis was hurt or dead. Jesus, would he ever be in for the surprise of his life.

Luis rolled over and picked up the phone, dialed Crothers' number. He wasn't home, but a machine picked up.

"Hey, partner," Luis said, "you gotta help me out. Turns out I'm pretty sick after all. The doctor wants me to fly up to 'Frisco to see this specialist. Do me a favor and tell the captain I'm going to be gone for longer than I thought. Thanks, man. You're a pal."

The call made, he finally fell asleep.

Two hours later he woke up from the dream, feeling an immense pressure in his head, like his brain was swelling, trying to break through his skull, seeking out possible escape routes. His eyes, his ears, his nose. Everything felt full, crammed, suffocated. He couldn't breathe.

Luis rolled to his feet and ran to his car, passing the check-in girl on the way out. She cowered behind the counter as he ran by.

Back in the Mustang, the pain in his head subsided enough that he could drive, though it still lingered there, urging him on, faster, faster.

He took the ramp to the interstate, making sure to keep his speed reasonable. The last thing he needed now was to get pulled over for a speeding violation.

Twenty minutes later he crossed the border into Maine.

This is it, he thought, this is where she is. Luis didn't know where the thought had come from, but he didn't question its merit. The girl from his visions was close. She was in Maine.

A green exit sign for Kittery whipped by, and Luis smiled. He knew he was close now. He could feel it. And in his heart he felt the sudden certainty that all he had to do to get his life back was kill one brown-haired girl, and that was fine by him.

Chapter 14

Steve Crothers stopped in front of Argento's door and checked the scrap of paper in his hand to make sure he had the right apartment. Number 212, Santa Rosa Apartments: the address he'd copied down from Argento's file at the station. This was it.

He knocked. There was no answer, and that actually took Crothers a little by surprise. In the back of his mind, he'd half-expected, and half-hoped, to be perfectly honest, that Argento would come to the door dressed in nothing but boxers and a rumpled T-shirt, a can of warm beer in one hand and a bag of chips in the other, the Raiders pre-game show on the TV in the background, and that would have been okay with Crothers. That would have been just peachy.

As far as Steve Crothers was concerned, there was nothing wrong with taking a few days' sick leave for some R&R, or even just to get off the streets for a while, but this was no normal situation. This was Luis Argento, who never missed a day, who had never, in the more than five years they'd been partners, been late even once to work, and that was what really made Crothers nervous. Not because Crothers thought Argento might be really sick, holed up and dying in his apartment, but because, when you came right down to it, Argento gave him the heebie-jeebies, and always had, since day one.

There was something strange about the man, just a bit off. The way he was always perfect, not so much as a hair out of

112

place, never saying the wrong thing at the wrong time, the way every human being is bound to do at least once in a while, never doing so much or so little as to call attention to himself. It disturbed Crothers, who may not have been a rocket scientist, but who wasn't stupid, either. It made him suspicious; the way Argento behaved seemed to Crothers the act of a man hiding something. If they'd been married, and a partnership on the force was a sort of marriage, really, Crothers would have thought Argento was having an affair. That possibility out, Crothers' mind naturally turned to other lines of reasoning. But not so different.

Crothers thought the most likely explanation for Argento's odd behavior was that he was on the take from someone. Maybe a dealer, one of the biggies down at the docks or in the city, or maybe one of the several mob-hands Crothers knew still operated in the city. It would explain his perpetual pursuit of inconspicuousness; a dirty cop wasn't one who wanted to be noticed, not even for good things.

Being a cop in L.A. was hard fucking work, the kind that only earned you so much money. Crothers knew a lot of good men who'd gone down for taking a cut from someone to turn a blind eye, and he knew a lot of other guys who'd been doing the same thing for years but hadn't been touched for it. But Crothers was an honest cop, a hardworking cop with a job he loved, and he'd be damned if he was going to go down because of something his lousy, and often creepy, partner was into. No way in hell.

There were other possibilities, too, of course. Argento could really be sick, or maybe there was trouble in his family he needed to take care of, but he didn't feel like dealing with the counseling sessions the department would inevitably saddle him with. Or maybe he was shacked up inside with an entire harem of prostitutes, fucking his brains out. Any of those things would have been fine, but if Argento was on the take, he wasn't going to drag Crothers down into the toilet with him.

Crothers banged on the door again, harder this time, rattling the thick, wooden slab in its frame. Still no sound from inside.

Fuck this. If Argento was home, prostitutes or no, he was about to get one hell of a surprise.

Crothers slipped a small leather bundle from his jacket pocket and rolled it open, exposing a number of lock-picks of various sizes and shapes. He looked at Argento's lock, made a quick mental measurement, and then pulled two of the picks from their sleeves. He glanced down the hall, which was open to the street behind him, saw nobody in the area, and inserted the picks, one in the top of the lock, one in the bottom. He jiggled the bottom, twisted the top hard to the right, felt the tumbler go, and quickly turned the knob and slipped inside Argento's apartment, shutting the door behind him.

He gagged and nearly vomited from the smell, rich and fruity, the stench of decomposition.

In one instant Crothers knew that the problem wasn't that Argento was on the take, and in that same moment wished fervently that he was. Crothers covered his nose with one hand and slipped his Glock 17 from its holster beneath his left armpit.

It was almost completely dark inside the apartment, but there was no sound. Crothers thought he was alone, felt alone, but kept the pistol unholstered. He was taking no chances.

Taking his hand away from his nose and mouth, holding his breath, Crothers groped along the wall to the right of the door, searching for the light switch with his free hand. He found it and flicked it up.

The overhead blinked on.

"Oh man, oh Jesus," he said to nobody, feeling light-headed, a brief storm of static washing over his vision.

He regained himself and plucked the radio-handset from his belt and called for backup, keeping his voice low. When he was finished, he put both hands back on the Glock, cupping his left under the right for support.

"Argento!" he said loudly. "You here?" No reply. Okay, Crothers told himself, okay, do it by the book. A quick search of the premises to make sure he's not hiding in the closet or under the bed, then get the hell out of here and wait for the troops to arrive. He stepped forward into the living room.

The room was chaos, bloody chaos. A T-shirt, once white but now stained a splotchy brown with dried blood, was thrown over the back of the couch. More bloody clothes—jeans and what looked like a blue blouse, badly torn—were piled in a corner. The walls were spattered with reddish-brown, slashed with it in long lines that reached the ceiling. Crothers had seen those sorts of lines on walls before and guessed that they were the result of a cut artery, probably carotid or femoral. When excited, the human heart can pump blood one hell of a ways.

The carpet in the room, Crothers surmised from the sole corner which had somehow been spared from the blood-bath, had once been white, but now it was a mess of red and brown, more red toward the center, where the blood was pooled thickly and less than completely dry. The blood there was no longer quite liquid, but hadn't yet caked hard and solid, either. He thought that if he were to touch it with a finger, it would feel a lot like finger-paint, thick and sticky and cold.

He moved into the kitchen, which was just off the living room, his Glock raised in front of him, right hand on the grip, left hand cupped beneath the right to steady his aim, ready to pump a fast ten rounds into anything that moved.

The kitchen was empty, neat and in order. Even the dishes had been done. Apparently the living room was for play and the kitchen was for quiet time. Crothers was heading back out and toward the back of the apartment when he noticed the wooden cutting board and what was on it. It was a thumb, sitting in a very round pool of congealed blood. The nail of the severed thumb was painted with blue nail polish, on top of which a small moon and star had been painted with silver polish. The long butcher's knife with which the digit had apparently been severed lay on the cutting board, too, its blade shiny at the edge in the glare of the overhead light.

He found Kim in the bathroom on the floor, naked, lying on her back in the middle of a clear plastic tarp.

The dead girl's pale body was covered with tattoos, and she was pierced in every conceivable place. A runaway, he thought, or a college kid. Crothers assumed from the relative lack of blood on the sheet that the blood splashed all over the living room was hers. What little blood was left in her body had settled down into her back and butt and the backs of her legs, all of which Crothers could see were a livid shade of purple.

From the look of her body, she'd been there some time, at least a few days. The corpse was bloated with the gas created by the bacteria in her body dissolving her tissues, not something which happened immediately after death. Round, bulging blisters, some of which had broken open from too much pressure, covered the surface of her skin, and clear fluid had trickled from her nose and mouth and from the corners of her eyes, pooling on the sheet. To his horror, Crothers realized the fluid was leaking from the dead girl's vagina as well, and had to swallow a mouthful of sour-tasting vomit.

He found the tubs in the bedroom, two of them, side by side, next to the bed, both set up high atop cinderblocks. There were blue, rounded plastic covers over both of them, concealing what was inside.

Gripping his gun tightly, finger on the trigger, Crothers kicked the top off the first one. It flew across the room and clattered to the ground near the closet door, which was open and empty. He stepped closer and peered into the tub. Empty. He moved to the next tub, repeated the process, sending the cover flying against the wall on the far side of the room. His heart was hammering in his chest. He edged closer.

There was someone inside, but it wasn't Argento.

This time Crothers couldn't hold it in and he fell to his knees, getting puke all over his pants and the front of his shirt.

The thing inside the tub was barely recognizable as human. The skin had burst open in long, ragged cracks and the flesh and muscle and fat inside had started to leak out, a light pink jelly which ran down into the bottom of the porcelain tub in a pasty stream.

Underneath the tub was a clear plastic bag, half-full of the pink glop, a disposal bag for the remains, so all Argento would be left with in the end was bones. Crothers saw that the bag was attached to the tub via a length of green garden hose.

In the distance he heard sirens.

Crothers was still on his knees when they found him and led him outside to a cruiser, where he stripped off his soiled shirt and put on a gray department sweatshirt someone tossed his way.

From inside the apartment, even from the parking lot of the complex, he could hear the sounds of retching. Although he wanted to and felt he should, Crothers found that he couldn't bring himself to go back inside the apartment, so he walked to his car and sat on the hood, smoking a cigarette.

Forty-five minutes later, though, he found that he'd gone through half a pack of Camels and was beginning to feel himself again.

"Detective Crothers?" he heard, and looked up. It was a young uniform, a kid Crothers recognized but couldn't put a name to.

"Yeah."

"I think you might want to go up there. They found some things."

Bracing himself, Crothers dropped his latest butt to the ground and crushed it out with his heel, noting, as he headed for the stairs to the second floor of the complex, that the young uniform was in no hurry to follow.

It wasn't as bad as he'd feared.

Yellow tape now cordoned off the area, and that in itself did something to numb Crothers to what he knew he was going to see. It's one thing to walk onto a crime scene where people have been before you, no matter how atrocious the crime might have been. It's a different animal altogether to be first man on, not knowing what to expect.

As he walked in the door, someone waved to him from the kitchen. Frank Pirelli, a detective from the West Hollywood Precinct. Crothers hadn't seen him arrive, but then, he'd hardly been in the most observant of modes when the cavalry had shown up.

"What's up?" he said, walking over.

Pirelli had latex gloves on and was holding something, a brown leather bag about the size of a notebook, gingerly by the corners. The zipper had been opened, and inside Crothers could see what looked like the tops of Polaroid photographs.

"This guy was your partner, right?" Pirelli said, and Crothers could see a kind of sympathy in his eyes. He knew how hard this was going to be for Crothers to live down. Something like this could end a career.

"Six years, man. Six goddamn years."

"Don't that beat all," the detective said. "You never knew anything was up with this weirdo?"

Crothers chuckled grimly. "Sure," he said, "I knew the whole time, but I've got this mushy soft spot for serial murderers, Pirelli. Always gets me into trouble. Maybe I'm in the wrong line of work, huh?"

"That's funny, Steve. Really, you should be a comedian or something. Anyway, I thought you might want to take a look at this."

Crothers pulled a pair of latex gloves from a paper slip in his back pants pocket and put them on, then took the leather bag from the other detective.

At first glance, he thought there must be at least fifty photographs inside the pouch. As it turned out, there was no need to count. On the back of the first picture he pulled out was a number in black marker and a name, along with a date: 41 KIM 1-17-99. He turned the picture over and saw a girl, recognizably the one lying on the floor of the bathroom, standing inside the door of the bedroom in her bra and panties, smiling widely, completely oblivious to what was about to happen to her.

Being careful not to disturb the order the pictures were in, he pulled out the next one in the sequence. Same girl, naked to the waist, exposing her generously tattooed torso, small breasts limp against her gaunt ribcage, a far cry from the bloated thing in the bathroom now. In the next picture she was down on the floor of the living room—Crothers could tell from the white carpet which had still, at that point, been white—a large knife deep in her chest, blood seeping out of at least five other gashes in her neck and chest area.

The next series, three pictures again, these all with the number 40 and JACK scrawled on the backs, were of a boy with crew-cut blond hair, maybe fifteen years old, dressed in ratty jeans and an AC/DC T-shirt. Smiling. Naked. Dead. Strangled with what seemed to be a length of black phone cord, twisty like a pig's tail, and stabbed at least half a dozen times in the stomach and chest.

Crothers wondered if Jack was the thing melting in the tub.

He leafed through the rest of the photos, his horror and revulsion growing with every new image.

The apartment was the setting of most, but not all, of the pictures. Some were in alleys, or in other rooms Crothers didn't recognize. Nor were they all of children. At least half of the people in the pictures were adults. Men, women, children, dates going back almost ten years. There were first names on most, but not on all, of the Polaroids, and even last names on a few.

There was only one break from form in the organization of the Polaroids. Just after Jack, the kid in the AC/DC shirt, there were three blank sheets of white paper that had been cut to match exactly the dimensions of the pictures. Written on the small rectangles were, MOM, DAD, SONNY BOY. Apparently Argento had been without his camera that night.

Crothers zipped the pouch back up and dropped it into an evidence bag, then looked around for Pirelli and found him barking orders near the door and drinking a cup of coffee from a Dunkin' Donuts cup. Crothers' stomach growled hungrily; he'd lost everything he'd eaten for breakfast back in the bedroom.

"I'm going to take this to Unsolved," Crothers said. "I

want to get the victims ID'd ASAP. Is there an APB out on Argento?"

"Had it out half an hour ago."

"Good, but I don't think he's anywhere local. Last time I talked to him, he mentioned that he was going to San Fran to see a doctor or something. Let's get this out over the wire, too. I don't think he's in town; otherwise, I think he would have been here. Guys like this don't like to leave their pads for long, and from the looks of it, he's been gone for a while. Could be he's on the run; maybe something spooked him. Might be a good idea to put something out nationwide about Argento's MO. Mention knives. That seems to be his thing."

"Could be he's out looking for forty-two," Pirelli said. "Maybe he'll just come home tonight."

Crothers looked around at the bloodstained ruin that was his partner's apartment. "Maybe. But I don't think so."

Chapter 15

Cora came to a stop, panting. Her left arm was throbbing. The pain was sharp and breath-sucking. She felt hot and a little bit insane with it, as though any moment she might start laughing and not be able to stop.

In front of her, Cedar Avenue sloped sharply away into darkness. Another road, Walnut Lane, intersected it here, heading off to her right and dead-ending on her left. Right, she knew, was the Bridgewater Mall, but that was almost a mile away. Left, through the backyard of the house she stood next to, was the college, not of much use to her now.

She needed someplace to hide out, someplace to rest. She was exhausted, and didn't know how much longer she could stay ahead of him. He was already getting too close. Just a few minutes ago, he'd almost caught her in town. She'd only managed to escape by hopping from the second-story balcony of The Inglenook, a restaurant her parents had taken her to once. Landing, she'd slipped and fallen hard, jamming her elbow into the concrete, sending electric pulses up and down the left side of her body. That had gradually faded into the current numb throb.

Come on, she thought, *slow down. Breathe. Think. Where are you? What are your options?*

Not the mall. Having some people around was good, since it helped distract the dark man, but that had backfired on her before. Too many stimuli were hard to deal with, and once she'd almost walked right into his arms outside American Eagle. Enormous as he was, she hadn't even seen him.

The college was no good, either. She'd gone to that well too often in the beginning, and now he knew the layouts of the buildings on campus almost as well as she did. Then where?

Straight ahead, at the bottom of the hill, the Crum Woods began. But Cora didn't want to go in there. Not at night. Not ever. The only memories she had of the woods were bad ones.

Then she had it. Her friend Helen's house. It was only about a block away, and she'd never hidden there before.

Feeling the first hint of relief, Cora turned back the way she'd just come and just managed to evade the razor that sliced at the air in front of her face.

Letting out a strangled scream, she stumbled backward and her feet got tangled up. She fell and rolled backward as a black-booted foot launched itself at her head, barely missing with what would have been a skull-cracking blow.

In half a second she was back on her feet, the pain in her arm forgotten.

The dark man came at her, razor held out down at his right side. Cora moved to her right and he moved to his left, circling her, but closing, always closing.

He lunged with the razor and barely missed Cora's bad arm. She searched the darkness behind him, looking for an escape route. He came again, swiping wide with the razor to push her left, then lunging for her with his left hand, trying to grab her arm. She ducked right and down, and all he came away with were a few strands of hair.

Now he was circling again, moving to his right. He was very close now, just three or four feet from her. Behind him, Cora saw a dark gap in the curb on the far side of the road. A drainage grate for runoff.

So preoccupied with the grate was she that he almost managed to wrap his arms around her as he lunged again with both arms, trying to catch her into a bear-hug.

Thinking fast, she ducked beneath his embrace and rolled past him, then bolted to her feet and sprinted in the direction of the grate. As she got closer, she saw that the tarmac of the street had overrun the lip of the grate, sealing the metal top of the drainage grate down. No dice there. She turned and looked for the dark man, certain that he would be right behind her. But he was nowhere to be seen.

It was only when she heard the cracking of twigs from the hedges bordering the sidewalk that she realized he'd circled her again. But by then it was too late.

He burst from the hedges just a couple of feet from her and swung hard with his free hand, connecting with the side of Cora's head. Gasping in pain, she toppled to the ground, striking her chin hard on the road. She lay still there, unmoving.

The dark man approached her, nudged her legs with a foot. Satisfied that she was incapacitated, he leaned over toward her.

Summoning everything she had left, Cora kicked with both feet at the dark man's ankles, sweeping them out from under him. He fell backwards, hitting the ground with a solid thunk. Cora took advantage of the opening, climbing quickly to her feet and taking off down the street in the direction of Helen's house.

Halfway down the block she looked back over her shoulder. He was on his feet and moving. He's too strong, Cora thought. He's too fast. I can't keep on doing this.

It was all she could do to keep her feet moving.

Chapter 16

Cole woke to the smell of coffee and the sounds of cooking. He sat up and peered bleary-eyed over the back of the couch, where he'd slept, surrendering the bed to Sarah again.

Back snapping and crunching with an enthusiasm Cole just knew couldn't be healthy, he stood and walked to the kitchen.

He found Sarah, dressed in his old red-and-black-striped terrycloth bathrobe, long hair tied back away from her face in a ponytail, working up a batch of scrambled eggs, wooden spatula in one hand, a cup of strong black coffee in the other.

"Well, good morning," he said. He got a mug and poured himself a cup of coffee, then added a generous glug of milk and an even more generous spoonful of sugar. "This sure brings back the memories, doesn't it?"

"I was just thinking that," Sarah said, "but wasn't it usually you who made the breakfast?" There were discolored, purplish blotches under her eyes and her face looked pale and drawn. Cole wondered if it was physical or mental fatigue, or both. Either way, she looked ten times better than she had the night before, when her breathing had been so shallow that Cole wasn't so certain that he shouldn't take her to the emergency room in Portland.

"How do you feel?" Cole said, taking the spatula from Sarah and motioning for her to sit down at the folding card table, which also doubled as his dining-room table and desk.

"Better than I look."

"I hope so, because you look like death, minus the whole warmed-over bit."

"I'd forgotten what a charmer you could be, my dear."

Grinning, Cole said, "The great ones never lose it, but only get better and better with the years, like a fine wine."

"Right." Sarah sipped her coffee.

Cole finished the eggs and doled them out, setting one plate in front of Sarah. He opened the refrigerator and grabbed the ketchup, dumped a pool of it on his plate, then sat down at the table.

"Eugh." Sarah grimaced, watching Cole dip his first forkful of egg in the ketchup. "I never could understand how that could possibly taste good."

"Your loss. So, tell me what happened yesterday."

As they drank coffee and ate their eggs, Sarah told Cole everything: about the deserted town she'd found herself in at first, about meeting Cora, about the man who had chased them through Cora's memories, the man who Cora said had killed her parents and brother.

When Sarah finished, she noticed Cole looking at her strangely, as though something was bothering him. "What are you thinking?" she said.

"Well, for one thing, doesn't it seem a little odd to you that her mind has taken on, from what you've told me, the attributes of a physical landscape?"

Sarah nodded. "I was surprised, too. For a few minutes I was completely disoriented. Everything was so real-looking, convincing. I told you that I'd done this once before. The last time was nothing like this. It happened in Philadelphia a couple of years ago. A man heard about me through a colleague and contacted me. He wanted me to ascertain the mental condition of his mother, who was comatose and in the hospital on life-support. He told me that he loved his mother very much, but if her brain was dead and there was no chance she would ever come out of her coma, then he wanted to pull the plug and let her die peacefully. So I did it."

"What was it like?"

"There's no way of describing it other than to say that I heard his mother's voice very faintly in my head, telling me that she was still there, somewhere way back where nobody would ever be able to find her, and that she wanted to go. But that's all it was, just a voice, more an impression, really. Nothing else, nothing like last night."

"So, why the difference?" Cole had a feeling that Sarah had already given this a good bit of thought and knew, or thought she knew, more than she was saying. "Come on, lay it on me."

"Okay," she said, "I'll tell you what I think, but first you have to tell me something."

"Shoot."

"Is the name of Cora's hometown in California Bridge-water?"

"How did you know that?" As far as he knew, Sarah had never seen Cora's file, and he was pretty sure that the name of the town hadn't come up in conversation.

Sarah blew out a breath, then let it fly. "Have you ever heard of a mind palace?"

Cole shook his head.

"It's basically just a very organized and efficient way of storing immense amounts of information in the mind," Sarah said. "People have been doing it forever. You construct your palace the way you want it and assign memories or informa-tion to different rooms or objects, and then when you want to remember something, all you have to do is go to that place or touch the object you've associated the information with, and it comes back to you just how you tucked it away."

"And you think that's what Cora's done, created one of these palaces in her mind?"

"I'm saying it's a possibility. It would make sense, wouldn't it? I mean, what better place to use for her palace then her hometown, where so many things happened to her, from where she has so many pleasant memories? If I were running from someone, I'd choose a place I was intimately familiar with, too. Wouldn't you? It gives her the edge, at least for a while."

"So she's hiding away in her memories from reality?"

Sarah shrugged. "Don't know. All I do know is that I have to go back in there, Cole, and soon. I have to bring her out, or something bad is going to happen."

"But why? You just finished telling me that she's hiding away inside her mind, living inside her memories. What could be more safe? Maybe she'll just come out when she's ready to face the world again, when she's dealt with the loss of her family. If what you say is true, then it sounds like a classic shock-induced coma. When her mind has dealt with what it needs to, she'll wake up. The coma is just her body's way of giving her time to heal."

"It's more serious than that," Sarah said, "much more. When I was in there last night, I fell down and scraped my hands on the gravel, and it hurt, Cole, it really hurt. And when I woke up this morning, I could hardly move. It felt like I'd just run five miles, and then I remembered that I did. Last night. Inside Cora's mind."

"That could just be from all the adrenaline you must have secreted last night. It's not that uncommon to wake up sore and stiff from nightmares, especially really active ones."

Sarah nodded. "That's true. But what about this?" She put her hands on the table, palms-up. The heels of her hands were scraped and red. "If you look nice and close, you can still see some of the little pieces of gravel that got under the skin." She could see him looking for words, for an explanation he could accept.

"That could have—"

"Could have what? Happened somewhere on the way back here? You carried me all the way back, right?"

Cole nodded. "Yeah, I did."

"Did you drop me anywhere? Did I ever touch the ground at all?"

"No."

"Then don't try to explain this away, Cole. This is real. Whatever's happening inside that little girl's head, she's powerful enough that she's managed somehow to make that real, too. I don't know how, and I don't know why, but it is. Do you understand that? Do you believe what I'm telling you?"

After a moment of silent contemplation, Cole said, "I guess I have to, don't I?"

"If we're going to save that girl's life, then yes, you do. She's not alone in there. She's in real danger, and not just from the coma."

"You mean the man who chased you? But even if all of what you've said is true, he's still nothing more than Cora's memory of the man who killed her family. He's not really dangerous. She just thinks he is. That's what gives her coma the power it needs to hold her. The fear."

Sarah tried to control the impatience that was bubbling up inside her. She knew that Cole had always been a reasonable person, a scientist in the truest sense, dependent on facts and numbers, things he could see and prove, or otherwise disbelieve as the stuff of imagination, hallucination. This was a luxury Sarah, because of the nature of her gift, had never in her adult life been able to afford herself. For her, the truth very often lay in a hunch, or in an image, something there and then gone again, like smoke in the wind. It was this sort of feeling she had about the man in Cora's mind palace, and she knew beyond question that she was right.

"I don't think he is a manifestation of her imagination," she said, taking care to keep her voice calm and neutral. "Cora thinks that he's a . . . a relic of the man who killed her family, a sort of remnant of the killer's psyche, left to finish what the real, physical killer couldn't. I think she might be right."

The look on Cole's face was skeptical. "But how could that happen?"

"I don't know," Sarah said. "Maybe it was something about the emotional height of the moment. Maybe as she was watching her family being slaughtered, her mental defenses dropped and his rage and hate were imprinted on her, like a stamp on paper. Maybe it was as involuntary for him as it was for her. Either way, the important thing is that she says he's getting stronger, more difficult to evade. We have to get her out of there, Cole. Somehow." No longer willing to debate the issue, Sarah pressed her side. "When's the soonest you can get me back there?"

Cole appeared to consider her question for a moment. Inside his head, Sarah could almost hear the thoughts conflicting with one another, bumping and crashing in a confusing jumble. In the end, as she'd known it would, his faith in her won out. "How does tonight sound?"

Sarah nodded. "Tonight it is," she said, then stood and arched her back, hands on her hips, shoulders pushed far back. There was a series of snaps from her spine and she sighed with obvious pleasure.

She held out a hand to Cole. He took it in one of his own and rose to his feet.

"What's this?" he said as Sarah pulled him out of the kitchen and toward the bedroom.

"It's going to be tiring tonight," she answered. "We need to catch up on our sleep."

Cole grinned. "But I just woke up. I'm not tired anymore."

This time it was Sarah's turn to smile. "Don't worry," she said. "You will be."

Chapter 17

Something was nagging at Crothers, something about the crime scene, Argento's apartment. He felt as thought he'd missed something so obvious, something right in front of his face. It wouldn't have surprised Crothers terribly if he had, either, not in his current state of mind. Some of the things going through his mind . . . Christ, they just had no place in a cop's thought process. Still, they were there, and they were making a lot of sense to Crothers right about now.

Broken down into its most elementary terms, somewhere between Argento's place and the station, Crothers had, quite simply, decided that Argento was going to die. What's more, Crothers had decided that he was going to be the one doing the killing. There was simply no alternative in the matter.

Once he'd managed to get past the initial shock of discovering that his partner of several years was one of the most active serial predators in the country, Crothers had realized he needed some time to really consider the matter. Fortunately, the paperwork he was required to write up detailing his discovery of Argento's lair provided him with just such an opportunity.

Looking through Argento's photo collection, Crothers had really begun to feel the rage building inside him, gathering in his gut like blood from a ruptured organ. And in some very important way, he did feel ruptured.

Many of the faces from the collection Crothers recognized

as cases he and Argento had worked together. Missing person cases mostly. And that smug, calculating bastard had known all along what had happened to them, that they were never going to be found. He knew because they were back in his apartment, dissolving in tubs. God Almighty. It didn't feel real.

How could someone he'd known for so long, someone he'd worked with every day for years, have fooled him so completely? What did that say about him? As a cop? As a person? It was almost too much to think about.

He stood up and paced in front of his desk, which he did when he had to do some serious thinking. Twenty minutes later, he had nothing but an ache in his right knee.

He decided to take a drive.

The scene had cleared at Argento's, but the yellow tape was still up around his door and would be for days, Crothers knew. He let himself into the apartment and stood inside the open doorway, waiting for inspiration to strike.

He was almost surprised when it did.

The answering machine light was blinking. Crothers pulled his handkerchief from his pocket and, sheathing his finger in the fabric, pushed the playback button.

The tape rewound and then clicked automatically into play.

"Got your message, Argento," Crothers' own voice issued from the machine, tinny and hollow. "Hope everything works out in 'Frisco. I'll tell the chief what you said. Talk to ya." Click.

Invigorated, he rushed out of the apartment and down to his car.

Back at the station, he sat down and picked up the phone and dialed a zero.

"Operator," a woman's voice answered after half a ring.

"This is Detective Steven Crothers of the LAPD," he said. "I need you to tell me where two calls to my home were placed from. Can you do that?"

The operator asked him for his home phone number and the date the calls were placed, and in less than five minutes, Crothers had the names of the places Argento had called him from: the first from a joint called TJ's Diner in Kansas City, Missouri, the second from a Holiday Inn in Portsmouth, New Hampshire.

East, he thought, *the bastard's gone east.* He picked up the receiver of his desk-phone and punched in the extension for Dispatch. Someone female picked up on the first ring.

"Who's this?" Crothers said.

"Lieutenant Blaine."

"Okay, Blaine," Crothers said, "I need you to do some things for me. You got a pencil and paper ready?"

Chapter 18

Luis pulled the Mustang to a stop beneath a drooping, snow-coated pine and killed the engine.

The ensuing silence was absolute, save for the quiet sounds of his breathing. It was a shock to his ears, which for more than three days had been filled nearly constantly with the sounds of driving. The wind, the engine, the radio. The quiet was beautiful.

He opened the Mustang's door and stepped out of the car. As if on cue, it began to snow, lazy flakes drifting down. Or had it been snowing all along? Luis couldn't recall, but wouldn't have been surprised if it had been. This place seemed made for snow.

He'd arrived in Stone Beach about twenty minutes ago and had driven around until he found this spot, just outside the gates of a small cemetery. He'd also managed to get some scouting done and knew pretty well where he was. Town was a mile or so south, and about the same distance to the north was a cluster of expensive-looking beachfront homes. He'd noticed them from the interstate and had made a mental note.

Pushing his hands into his pockets, Luis headed that way now, north, leaning into the wind and snow, which were blowing directly against him. The snow was coming down more heavily now and Luis could only see twenty or thirty feet ahead. The world had turned suddenly the color of bone.

About half a mile later, the road Luis was following re-joined Coastal Route 2, which ran alongside the shoreline. Not very far away, Luis could see wispy fingers of gray smoke rising from amidst the trees on the coast-side of the highway, barely distinguishable from the whiteness of the swirling snow. He broke into a cautious jog, not wanting to slip and fall on the icy road, hands still jammed in his pockets.

After five minutes, he jumped the railing on the side of the road and slid on his ass down a small hill. In front of him, there was a shallow line of pine trees and, just on the other side of them, a six-foot chain-link fence defined the spacious rectangular backyard of a sprawling ranch-style house.

Luis moved toward the fence, ready to jump it, but a sound stopped him in his tracks. A throaty growl, like a diesel engine firing up.

A red dog trotted around the side of the house and into sight. It was wide in the shoulders and narrower in back, starred white on the chest, head long and straight, powerful-looking. Moving slowly through the snow, predatorily, it approached the fence, stopping no more than ten feet from where Luis stood on the other side.

"Shit," Luis said. He was cold, and getting colder every moment. His leather jacket was doing shit to block the wind, and his face was so cold it felt hot. His ears had hurt for a while, but now he felt them only in sharp flashes. Even if there had been another house right next door, Luis didn't think he'd have gone. It was this house he wanted, this house he needed. He knew that, but he didn't know why.

Barely thinking, moving quickly and somehow instinctively, Luis shucked off his jacket and folded it in two, then drew his Glock 17 from the holster beneath his arm. He covered the pistol with the jacket, then stepped forward.

The dog jumped toward Luis and reared up against the fence, breaking into a spasm of deep, throaty barking.

Luis stepped closer, until he was just a foot away from the animal, jammed the bundle containing the pistol up against the fence, and pulled the trigger twice in quick succession. SNAP-SNAP. The reports were muffled by the thick leather and sounded no louder than caps being exploded.

Luis reholstered his gun and shrugged his jacket back on, then climbed the fence and hopped to the ground on the other side.

He walked to the back door of the house, but it was locked and looked solid. From the way it didn't even budge when he pushed on the door, he assumed it was braced somehow from within.

As he was making his way around to the front of the house, he saw the boat. It was in the water, tied to the dock, bobbing crazily in the rough water.

He tore his eyes off it and continued toward the front door. Through the window on this left, he could see inside the house, into the living room. A man and a woman were sitting in recliners, watching TV. There was a fire going in the fireplace behind them. It looked warm, so warm.

Luis drew his gun again with a hand he could hardly feel and lurched toward the door. He stopped in front of it, wanting nothing more than to kick through it, kill the man and woman, and sit in their warm house until he was warm, too. He stepped back from the door, prepared himself to lunge forward . . . but he couldn't.

In his mind, he moaned in agony, begged, *"Please please please let me let me,"* but all that came out of his mouth was an inarticulate sound of pain and anger, more animal than human, the sound of an animal caught in a trapper's iron-foot.

He turned away from the door and stumbled toward the water, toward the motorboat.

In what must have been five minutes but felt like an hour, Luis was hundreds of yards from the house, heading into the center of the bay.

A big wave crashed into the boat and nearly flipped it, but Luis was able to throw enough of his weight to the other side to keep it from going over. The engine sputtered, and for a second Luis was afraid it was going to die; then it caught and buzzed back into life, clearing itself of water with a powerful shudder and a cloud of black, oily smoke.

Peering ahead into the curtain of snow, Luis could see practically nothing, only the grayness of the raging waters surrounding him, and the grayness of the sky above. The two were nearly indistinguishable. It was hard to tell where one started and the other began. He was prisoner in a world of lethal colorlessness, but the magnet in his head was pulling him along, and he had no choice but to trust it.

Another wave sideswiped the tiny vessel and it nearly went over again, catching Luis off-guard. He threw himself to the other side of the boat and his hand slipped on the icy side. He cracked his ribs hard against the wood, but again the boat righted itself.

Wave after wave of frigid water sloshed up over the side of the boat and drenched Luis. The water was unbelievably cold, and the feeling in his fingers and toes was beginning to fade. The engine sputtered again, and this time it did die, coughing its way to a dramatic demise.

Moving quickly, feeling panic circling him like a carrion bird, Luis stepped from the back of the boat into the middle and pulled the oars out from underneath the benches. He plugged them into the oarlocks. The oars were old and gray and Luis only hoped they wouldn't snap under the pressure of the furious ocean. He stroked, pulling with all of his strength, struggling to keep the boat pointed in the direction he somehow knew it needed to go, then again, and again, making adjustments without looking, ceasing his rowing only when he needed his hands and body to steady the boat.

After what felt like five hours, the hull scraped over something. He pulled again and the bow ground up on land. Luis climbed out, his back feeling as though it were on fire, and with Herculean effort dragged the boat far up on the rocky shore, out of the reach of the greedy waves.

About twenty yards from where he'd landed there was a thicket of pine trees, and Luis headed for it, shuddering so badly from the cold that he thought he was going to break right apart at the joints, the world's first crumbling man.

Other than the trees, not much was visible in any direction through the nearly impenetrable field of falling snow. Beyond the trees, Luis could just barely see the foot of a hill sloping up, a wide swath of darkness more than anything else. He followed it up with his eyes. From somewhere beyond the cusp of the hill, a bright light swept across the waters of the bay. The beam briefly illuminated the top of the hill, which had to have been at least a hundred feet high and rose almost straight up. There was no way he'd be able to climb it in his current state.

Once again his eyes honed in on the pine trees and he lurched that way, fighting to stay upright as slippery stones under his feet conspired to topple him.

The storm-drain *found* Luis more than the other way around, ramming him in the shins. It was about two and a half feet wide and set up off the ground atop a concrete abutment. Luis traced its path with his eyes and saw that it ran for about fifteen or twenty feet before disappearing into the hillside. Unthinking, knowing only that if he didn't get warm soon he was going to fall down and pass out, Luis hauled himself up and in and started moving: half-crawling, half-slithering, beginning to feel weak and lightheaded.

After a slow fifty or so feet, the pipe dead-ended, leaving Luis facing ahead toward a wall and no room to turn around. Near the end of his strength, he groped with one hand around the pipe in the darkness while supporting himself with the other. There was a grate above.

He worked his way onto his back and pushed up against it, but it wouldn't move. Panting, he let his arms drop to his sides.

That was it; there was nothing left. Nothing. His hands felt huge and leaden, like dumbbell weights, his arms like strands of spaghetti.

But he had come so far. And he was so close now, he could feel that.

Raising his arms again, he wrapped his numbed fingers around the bars of the grate and heaved upward, channeling every ounce of strength he possessed into the motion.

Something gave and the grate moved.

So exhausted now that he was crying with effort and pain, chest hitching with painful sobs, Luis slid the heavy metal grate away from the opening and, with the little he had left, squeezed up out of the pipe and onto the stone floor, where he lay, shaking. It was minutes before he found the strength to pull the little penlight from its slip in his belt.

Luis fought to his knees, then twisted the head of the small light until a narrow beam issued forth and then panned it around, revealing in bits and pieces the narrow room he had entered through the grate.

The walls were lined with cots up on end, mattresses torn to pieces on the floor. For the first time Luis smelled the fetid odor in the air and recognized it right away. Rat shit.

Beside each of the upended cots was a black footlocker.

Luis crawled over to the nearest one and pulled it open, holding the light between his teeth, shining it down on his hands. Empty.

He moved to the next and lifted the lid, revealing a blue blanket. In another he found, mixed in with a sheaf of yellowing paper and an old book, a musty blue T-shirt with U.S. NAVY printed across the chest.

Luis shucked off his wet coat and pulled his shirt off, then slid the dry, dusty T-shirt over his head and wrapped himself in the blanket. The dry shirt helped, as did the fact that it was warmer in here. There was heat coming from somewhere. From far off he thought he could hear the dull roar of a furnace.

Not wanting to kill the batteries in his penlight, he twisted the head of the little flashlight until it went off and lay in the dark on the hard floor, the only sounds the chattering of his own teeth, and the unmistakable squeaking of rats.

Chapter 19

Lying in bed next to Cole, her face no more than six inches from his face, Sarah felt an incredible mix of emotions, not the least of which was happiness. It was the first time in a long time she'd felt so close to bliss.

For longer than she cared to remember, Sarah had wondered what it would be like to be with Cole again. He'd been the last man, the only man she had loved, before her psychic abilities began to assert themselves. It had never been quite the same with anyone else afterward. Over the years she'd come to think of men as books, and Cole was the only man whose last line she didn't know before she'd even begun to read. Even now, there was still so much she didn't know about him.

She brought a hand up to Cole's sleeping face and ran her fingers over his forehead, stroked his eyebrows. He was hot and a sheen of sweat coated his skin. She wondered what he was dreaming about, and thought that maybe she already knew. But she wasn't sure, and that was hard for her.

She could know everything if she wanted to. She could know who the little boy was that she'd seen in flashes, the one she thought he was dreaming about even now, and how he figured into the great sadness emanating perpetually from Cole. And she could know what had happened between Cole and his wife, what had driven them apart. She could know everything.

And that had always been the problem. There was a part of Sarah which had never really gotten over Cole leaving her, though she had come to terms a long time ago with why he had done so. In a very real way, Cole's removal of himself from her life at just the point where she needed him the most had affected Sarah's ability to trust. Not just men, either, but anyone. But knowing that didn't change it.

After her relationship with Cole ended, it hadn't been difficult for Sarah to find men, even men she was interested in. Raleigh-Durham, and the rest of the Research Triangle, for that matter, was a meat-market for horny college and graduate students. After she and Cole had split, Sarah had tentatively stuck her toe down into those waters and tried out the bar and club scene.

Over the next couple of years, during which Sarah finished up her studies at Duke, she'd taken a short string of lovers into her bed, men she thought from her initial impressions she could trust not to hurt her, at least if she didn't let them.

For some time she had been studying psychic phenomena and had learned to erect mental barriers around herself, to protect her from the ferocity of people's thoughts, and that was what she chose to do with the men in her life.

No matter what anyone might say to the contrary, Sarah knew in a way few others could that the most painful thing in life was to know exactly what everyone around you was thinking: about you, about everything, all the time. It was a dirty, soiled feeling. But even worse than having to tolerate the thoughts in people's minds was knowing that, eventually, the people she cared about most would begin to hide themselves from her. She wasn't the only person in the world who knew how to build walls.

But for a while she had managed to be happy, or at least she thought she'd been happy. Her proficiency at blocking

143

the thoughts of others had reached a high enough level that she could almost remember what it was like to be normal again. But it had always ended here. In bed. In the hours after lovemaking, when she couldn't help herself anymore. It was just a precautionary measure, she had told herself time and time again. What was the use in wasting her time with someone, if she could know in seconds what they really felt and thought about her?

There was also something undeniably God-like about the power to know in mere seconds everything there was to know about someone, to insert herself into their minds and memories and let them wash over her like waves, to soak those things up, and then, very simply, to know. To know everything that made them who they were, the most powerfully defining things about them.

No door was closed for Sarah. During one of her psychic forays, she had discovered that the man sleeping beside her, whom she'd been seeing for nearly three months and who was brilliant in bed, had once murdered another man in the alley behind a bar in South Dakota with a broken off cue-stick, had beaten his skull with it until the hard bone lost its round shape and took on the consistency of lumpy paste. She knew that, just as she knew that he'd done it because the other man had looked a second too long at the legs of the girl he'd been seeing at the time when they walked into the bar together.

These were the things she knew, the things that she could know, and knowing just always seemed better than not.

Now here was Cole. Asleep on his side, face smooth and almost childlike. She had slept beside him like this hundreds of times in the past, but never before had she possessed the power to see into him, into the places he never showed anyone.

She raised her hand to his face and trailed her fingers

down from his temple, over his cheek, brushed her thumb softly over his lips, which were dry and warm, slightly parted. She could know. She could know everything.

Instead, she spoke.

"Cole." Her voice was weak because her throat was dry; his name came out of her mouth as little more than a whisper. She said his name again.

This time he opened his eyes, looked at her across the short, white expanse of pillow, a tired smile forming on his lips.

"Yeah?" He reached an arm out for her and pulled her closer, till their faces were only inches apart, till their bodies came together beneath the sheets.

"Can I ask you something? Something I'm afraid to ask, but need to know?"

She felt him tense against her, but he didn't show it in his face. "What?"

She was unsure of this. If she asked him, he would think she'd been snooping around his mind. He would be suspicious. He would start building walls around himself, protecting his innermost self from her. Only it wouldn't stop there. It never did. Soon he would realize that the only way to live normally again would be to leave her and—

Jesus Christ, she thought, cutting herself off in mid-thought, *stop it, Sarah. You're an hour into this thing and you're already treating it like a marriage! He knows you. Just tell him the truth and he'll understand.*

"I want you to tell me why you're so sad," she said. "I can feel it coming off you. Even though I try to block it, I get . . ."

"What?" he said.

"I get flashes."

"Of what?" He wasn't angry at her. He just looked tired.

"A little boy," she said, and met his eyes with hers. He

145

tried to hold her gaze, but couldn't, and looked away, down. "Who is he, Cole?" She asked the question gently.

"He is—he was my son. My son, Jimmy. He died on his fifth birthday, drowned in our pool during his birthday party. Nobody even noticed he was gone, and by the time anyone thought to look for him, he was . . . well." A great sob hitched up in Cole's chest and he let it out. There was a hysterical edge to it, and Sarah put her arms around his head, hugged his face against her shoulder. After a brief moment, Cole seemed to bring himself under control, and spoke again. "We thought he must have hit his head and fallen in," Cole said. "He was always a good swimmer. Jimmy loved the water, the ocean. That's why we got the pool in the first place."

"How long has it been?" Sarah said.

"Almost six years."

"I'm so sorry, Cole. So sorry." She kissed him on the forehead and he put his arms around her and hugged her tightly. His breath was warm against her neck, his lips almost hot, feverish. "Is Jimmy's death the reason you and Jessica divorced?"

"We tried to convince ourselves it wasn't, by hating each other for everything else in the world, but yeah. Yeah, it was." Cole's back began to hitch beneath Sarah's caressing hands, and she held him more tightly. It was only after a few seconds had passed that she realized he wasn't crying, but laughing!

"What is it?" she said, amazed.

"It's just—it's just that when—" He rolled onto his back and cut himself off with a gust of manic laughter.

"Well, what the hell's so funny?" Sarah said, laughing now too, in spite of herself.

Cole fought to get himself under control, then spoke again, a huge smile still on his face, a tear running from the corner of one eye. "God," he said, "I don't know why I'm laughing. It really isn't funny at all."

"What already?"

Cole took a breath and composed himself, then spoke. "When I came out of the house and found Jessica holding Jimmy, she was screaming and holding him really tightly. I wanted to do CPR, so I tried to take her off him, but she wouldn't let go, so I—I—" and he was off again, laughing, tears now streaming from his eyes and down over his cheeks.

When he could, he continued. "So, I tried to slap her across the face to get her to let go. But I missed. I hit her in the side of the head, instead. When the ambulance came, the paramedic said I'd given Jessica a severe concussion and popped her eardrum. Six months later, when she told me she wanted a divorce, that's the reason she had listed on the papers. Domestic violence."

Sarah and Cole locked eyes for a brief moment, and that was all it took.

They laughed until neither of them could breathe, but even then they couldn't stop. Several times they thought they had the fit beat, but then one or the other would let out a spontaneous snicker and it would all begin again.

The only thing that stopped their laughter in the end was sleep.

Sometime later, Sarah woke up to go the bathroom. It occurred to her that she and Cole had almost certainly missed the last ferry out to the Clinic, but it was only a few more hours until the morning ferry, and with everything that had happened in the last few days, they could use the rest.

When she returned to bed, she looked down at the man lying in it. And she felt hope. Real hope. It was something she thought she'd lost the capacity for. If he can laugh, he can heal, she thought.

She lay back down and pulled the sheets over herself, inched closer to Cole.

There was a strange tingling in her brain, and suddenly a familiar voice filled her head.

"Sarah! Help me!"

It was Cora. She was—

Flash.

Sarah felt herself being sucked away from the bed and Cole. She just barely had time to register—

Chapter 20

Steve Crothers hated flying. Not that he always had; there'd been a time where it hadn't fazed him one bit to step onto an airplane and strap himself in, but that was a long time ago. As his phobia had grown over the past ten or fifteen years, since about the time he graduated from Haverford College in Pennsylvania, Crothers had convinced himself that he was afraid because nobody could fly as many times as he had and escape without their number being called. The shuttling back and forth between Philadelphia and Los Angeles, where his family lived, had gradually instilled in him a crippling fear of flying. Where he had used to be certain that he would die by drowning, a conviction formed early in his childhood, Crothers was now convinced that he would die on a plane. But getting onto this one had been easy. Thoughts of death had never even entered his mind. Not of his own death, anyway.

Though on the surface of his consciousness Crothers told himself he was going to Maine to apprehend Argento and bring him back to L.A., deeper down, in the basest part of himself, he knew differently. He wasn't going all this way to toss a pair of cuffs on the motherfucker and drag him back to the California court system, which would indubitably find him insane and let him off with a life sentence. Crothers was going to Maine to do one thing, and one thing only. He was going to kill Argento. He was going to kill Argento, because

Argento had made him look like the worst kind of fool. Six years they'd been partners, and all that time Argento had successfully kept the truth from Crothers. All that time. Fucking Jesus H. Christ. Just thinking about it made Crothers' blood pound in his skull. Yeah, he'd kill Argento. He'd have no problem killing that psychotic son-of-a-bitch. He'd be doing the world a big favor.

Not that he would shoot him in cold blood. Crothers wasn't a murderer. But he didn't think it would come to that. Argento wouldn't surrender, not to Crothers, not to anyone. Argento would go down blazing, and that was fine. He'd lose. It was charitable, really, what Crothers was doing. Better to be dead than to be a cop in jail. Though the thought of Argento in jail, bunked up with the murderers and perverts he'd been putting away for the better part of a decade, made Crothers smile.

He shifted in the tight seat of the TWA 747 and tried for the twentieth time to straighten his cramped legs out. All he was successful in doing was eliciting an irritated look from the poofy blond in the seat in front of him.

"Blow it out your ass," Crothers muttered under his breath, but loud enough that he knew she'd hear. He was rewarded with an outraged grunt and saw the woman lean over to whisper to the man sitting next to her. The man, a balding dork of maybe fifty years, raised his head to look over the back of his seat. Crothers smiled beatifically back and said, "Can I help you, cueball?" The man promptly turned away and sat back down.

Still uncomfortable but feeling slightly better, Crothers pulled the phone from the seatback in front of him, making sure to jolt it harder than he needed to. He punched in his credit card number, then dialed the station in L.A. Blaine picked up.

"Blaine. Crothers. Anything yet?"

"Actually, yeah."

This took Crothers almost by surprise. "Well, what?" He had a bad feeling about what he might hear.

"Almost as soon as the APB went out on Argento's car, we got a hit in Maine. Town called Stone Beach. Sheriff there said the car was parked outside an old cemetery. It was covered with snow, so the patrolman who found it thought he'd take a look around inside, see if the driver'd collapsed or something. I guess it was really cold. No luck there, though, so he tagged the car as derelict and had it towed. Sheriff said the APB came in over the wire while he was going over the paperwork on Argento's car, or else he might have missed it totally. Lucky, huh?"

"Give me the number of the Stone Beach PD, wouldya?"

Blaine read Crothers the number. He thanked her and hung up, then dialed the number in Stone Beach, waited while the phone rang.

He'd been sure something would pop up eventually, but finding Argento's car was a surprise. Crothers' thinking had been more that he would get to Maine and then follow the trail of corpses to his partner. The car was a real break. It meant that Argento was close.

There was a click as the phone was picked up on the other end. "Stone Beach PD."

Crothers asked to be patched through to the sheriff, who was on patrol. In five minutes, he'd filled the man in on the situation and gotten directions to Stone Beach from the Portland Jetport.

He hung up the phone and sat back, pushing his legs out underneath the seat of the woman in front of him, jolting it hard. *Soon,* he thought, *soon.* He closed his eyes and tried to breathe slowly.

Chapter 21

Cora's voice spoke to Sarah out of the dark, whispered low.

"He's here, Sarah."

Sarah was cold, lying on her back in something soft and wet. It didn't help that she was wearing only her panties and the oversized white T-shirt she'd been wearing in Cole's bed.

She tried to sit up and got halfway there before striking her forehead hard on something solid maybe two feet above her.

"Ow!" she said, falling back onto her elbow, clamping a hand to her head. "Where the hell are we?" The darkness was deep. Sarah couldn't see anything at all. She heard her voice echoing distantly.

"In the sewer."

"In the what?"

"Don't worry, I know my way. My friends and I used to play down here when we were little."

"Why am I here?" It had just dawned on Sarah that Cora had pulled her inside her mind from miles away. *Jesus*, she thought, amazed. The power of Cora's mind was unbelievable.

Cora grabbed Sarah by the shoulders. Sarah's eyes were beginning to adjust to the darkness and she could faintly see the girl's outline hunched above her, though she couldn't make out her features.

"He's here," she said again, "I can feel him." Cora's voice was terrified, shaky. Sarah couldn't be sure, but it sounded like she was crying. What could have her so scared? Always before Cora had seemed anxious, but in control.

"If he's so close, why don't you find a memory to hide in?" Sarah said. "Like before?"

"No," Cora said, "not him, not *my* him. The real him! He's here, in the Clinic."

"What?" Sarah said, taken completely by surprise. "But your family was killed in California. Are you sure about this?"

"Yes."

"Oh my God." It made no sense. How could he possibly have known where she was? But that was unimportant. If Cora said that the man who had killed her family was on the island, then he must be. "Cora," Sarah said, already trying to figure out how long it would take to get from Cole's apartment out to the island, "you have to wake up. Right now."

This time there was no admonishing slap at the mention of her name. "I can't," Cora said. "I've already tried, but I can't do it. I can't wake up." There was panic in the girl's voice, and Sarah reached out with both hands and gently took Cora's face between her palms.

"Don't worry, sweetie," she whispered, "we'll figure this out. Just stay with me, okay? Hold it together for just a little longer." She could feel Cora shaking.

"Okay," Cora said, taking a deep breath.

Sarah suddenly had a thought. "The first time I came into your mind, it was over a bridge," she said, "at least that's where I remember waking up. Maybe that's a way out?"

"No," Cora said, "I've tried that. It just ends in the middle and drops off. That's not the way out, just the way in. But . . ." The girl's voice trailed off and she started to cry again.

"What is it, honey?" Sarah said. "Tell me."

Cora gathered herself and spoke. "It's not the way out, but

I think—I think it was once. I know it was. I've been looking ever since I got here, but there's no other way. None."

Sarah felt a cold, tight ball forming in her gut. Unreal, she thought. Impossible. "Are you saying that your world has changed since you got here?" But already it was starting to make sense to her.

"Yes," Cora said. "And not just the bridge. When I'm running from him, it's like the streets change. I'll turn down the road to my house and suddenly I'll be facing a dead-end, but a dead-end on the other side of town. It's like—"

"Like he is the one changing it." Sarah finished the girl's thought and Cora nodded, a brief bobbing of her outlined head in the gloom of the pipe.

And that was when two things became clear to Sarah, cold and shivering in her panties and a soggy T-shirt, squatting in an imaginary sewer-pipe. The first was that there was no way Cora would ever find the way out she was looking for, not the way she was going about looking for it; and the second was that Sarah thought she knew how she could help Cora find it. It was just a matter of asking the right questions.

"Okay," Sarah said, "if the way into your version of Bridgewater is over a bridge, what's the way out? What's your way out?"

"I don't know," Cora said, "I don't. I've tried everything, everywhere, every door, every road leading out of town. There's no way out. None!"

"Just relax," Sarah said. "I need you to think clearly for a second. Focus, kiddo. This is important."

"But there's no time. He's already here." In the girl's voice, Sarah could sense a fault-line, just beneath the surface, ready to split wide open. Still, it was do-or-die time now, and she couldn't afford to go slow. Who knew how close the killer was to Cora, how much longer she had before he found her helpless body bed-bound in the room at the Clinic. Frightened as she was for the girl's life, Sarah tried to keep the fear out of her voice. Cora didn't need to know how scared she was, too.

"Right now we need to worry about the things we can do something about," Sarah said. "We need to do this, and we need to do it now. Work with me, babe."

"But there is no way out, Sarah," Cora said, her voice rising hysterically. "That's the point. He's holding me here, so I can't wake up, so I'm helpless. There was a way out, but it's gone—"

"Bullshit, Cora. If there's a way in, there's a way out. That's just common sense. It's hidden, that's all. So well hidden, or so obvious, that you haven't been able to find it yet. Think. In Cora's world, in a world made of you, how do you find your way out when you're lost, when you're in trouble? Don't think about places the exit could be. Think about your experiences here, in this town. What's happened to you here where you had to find your way—"

Cora had been staring down, but now her head snapped up as something suddenly came to her. "Oh my God," she said, her tone disbelieving. "No way. That can't be it. Can't be. How could I have missed it all this time?"

"What?" Sarah said. "What is it?"

But Cora was already moving, crawling through the detritus gathered at the bottom of the pipe. Sarah lifted herself up onto her hands and knees and followed as quickly as she could. She had a feeling that if she lost Cora, the girl wouldn't stop to wait.

The pipe where Sarah had woken was only about ten feet long, and it dead-ended into a much wider one. Straightening up with a sigh, Sarah found that she could stand if she hunched over a little bit, and that was much preferable to crawling on her hands and knees through wet leaves and God only knew what else. Ahead, past Cora's fast-moving shape, Sarah could see the exit to the sewer, a small disk of gray in the deeper darkness. Night in nightworld.

The sewer pipe opened out halfway down the side of a steep, grassy hill. There was a huge expanse of water in front of them, and a small marina far below housed ten or fifteen gently bobbing boats, each moored to its own buoy. A concrete culvert ran the mile or so from where Cora and Sarah stood all the way down the hill and into the lake, a run-off for rainwater.

"Lake Kinneo," Cora said, pausing briefly to wait for Sarah to gather herself. "Come on." She turned and started hiking up the hill, leaning into the slope like a mountain goat, using her hands to grab handfuls of grass and dirt for support.

Sarah followed suit, thinking what an odd figure she must cut, wearing no pants or shoes, hiking up this hill in the middle of the night.

She caught up with Cora at the top of the hill.

"Wow," she said, trying to catch some breath. The entire town was spread out below them. Off in the distance, Sarah could make out the tall blue girders of the bridge she'd woken beside the first time she'd visited Cora's dream world.

"Where are we going?" Sarah said.

"You'll see," Cora answered, and Sarah could feel the fear in the girl's words.

They made their way down the hill and Cora led the way quickly through a residential section of the town. After a few minutes, the nearest of the shop fronts in the downtown area came into distant view, and past that Sarah could see the big ship-fountain, but Cora suddenly veered from the course they'd been holding and turned right, across the front lawn of a big old Colonial.

They passed by the house and over the lawn of the next, then crossed a street before heading down a long, sloping dead-end road. A few minutes later, they came to a stop in front of a thick growth of trees.

"Are we going in there?" Sarah said, searching for a path through the darkness of the trees, finding none.

Cora nodded. "We have to."

"Great." She couldn't blame Cora for being frightened. It looked pretty creepy in there.

Cora started into the woods, hands held out in front of her face to protect it from whipping branches.

As it turned out, there was a path, just a bad one. By the time the path finally decided to open up a little bit, Sarah's legs and arms were scratched and bleeding from a dozen places where branches and thorned weeds had raked her.

At a fork in the trail, Cora went right, downward. The other path went almost directly up. From ahead and below, Sarah could hear the sound of running water, faint, but unmistakable.

Not too much later, a fast-running river came into sight. Moonlight reflected off the water, making it sparkle. Cora stopped at the bank.

"Give me your hands," Cora said, holding her own out for Sarah, who took them and closed her eyes, waiting expectantly.

When she opened them it was still dark, but something was different. From all around there was noise. Birds chirped and things moved in the underbrush. A fish jumped in the river and splashed loudly back down. There was the throaty ribbiting chorus of many frogs.

Sarah turned to Cora and was startled to find that even she had changed. The girl was younger, maybe eleven or twelve, and wore denim shorts, a pink Izod shirt, and Birkenstock

157

sandals. Her brown hair was free around her shoulders. What really captivated Sarah about this younger version of Cora, though, were the girl's eyes, watery bright and saucer-wide. She looked absolutely terrified.

Cora released one of Sarah's hands, but kept her grip on the other, and began to walk along the bank of the river, where the trail ran, speaking as she moved. Though the girl looked much younger, the voice was that of the Cora Sarah knew.

"When I was a kid," she said in a voice just above a whisper, "my dad told me never to come down to the woods at night, but my friend Jackie lived on the other side and I used to cut through anyway, because it was faster than walking around. I did it for years, and I wasn't even scared, except of the noises I'd hear sometimes, but after a while I started wearing my Walkman, and then even that didn't bug me." She stopped talking long enough for both of them to hop over a downed tree across the path. "Then one night, while I was walking through, a bunch of older kids on dirt-bikes chased me off the trail and, when I ran away from them, I got lost. Lost."

The look on Cora's young face was haunted, terrified. Sarah thought that she was likely speaking more for her own sake than so that Sarah would understand what was happening. To their right, the river gurgled over rocks and around soggy, fallen trees. The sound of the water was peaceful, but it only put Sarah on edge. It was nearly impossible to hear the other sounds of the woods over the sound of the water.

Cora resumed speaking, her voice low, hushed. "I ended up down here by the river and hid for hours behind a big rock, just waiting for them to come back and find me. I thought they wanted to kill me. I know they did. I could feel it. I think that might have been the first time I really felt anything.

"Anyway, when I finally came out, I couldn't figure out which way to go. I'd never been so deep in the woods before, and it was really dark. And then I remembered something my dad told me once, when we all went on a trip to Yellowstone National Park. He said, 'If you ever get lost in the woods and find a river, follow it and it will lead you out. You may not be where you want to be, but at least you'll be out of the woods.' So I did. I followed this river."

From somewhere up ahead there was a dull, continuous sound, half-hiss and half hooded-roar. Sarah tried to place it but couldn't, even though it sounded familiar somehow.

"I came out in Jesop," Cora said. "Not where I wanted to come out, but out. I called my dad from a gas station and he came and picked me up." She stopped talking for a moment, but then added, "I came out, but not before they found me again. Not before they found me here."

The sound was louder now, and Sarah was beginning to understand what was making it.

"We used to come out here in high school, too, when I got older," Cora said. "Everyone did." Just ahead, Sarah could see a huge outcropping of rock: two enormous stones, one atop the other. "We called it Alligator Rock," Cora said, almost yelling now to be heard, "because the stones looked like an alligator's jaws. People would drink and do drugs up here. And some would jump."

Stepping up onto the outcropping, Sarah looked out over the river. "Shit," she whispered, but the word was smothered by the sound of the waterfall.

Below Alligator Rock, the riverbed fell away, straight down. It was impossible to tell how far, though, because the bottom of the falls was obscured by white mist. For all she knew, it could have been twenty-five feet, or a hundred.

Cora hopped up onto the rock and looked down, too. "I

was about to climb down when I heard the engines behind me," she said, and Sarah was just able to make out her words. "One of them revved his engine really loud and came shooting up here, and before I knew what was happening, I was in the water."

"Down there?" Sarah yelled, pointing at the bottom of the waterfall, disbelieving.

Cora nodded.

Oh man, Sarah thought, if she had to jump off this thing, she thought a heart attack would kill her even if the impact didn't, which it would.

"Does this feel like the way out?" she said to Cora.

The girl shrugged and shook her head, mouthed the words, "I don't know."

Sarah felt numb, terrified. There was no way to test this. If the way out was at the bottom of the waterfall, there was only one way to find out. It was do or die. Or, the cynical part of Sarah's mind chimed in, it was do *and* die.

She looked over at Cora, and found the girl looking back at her. They locked eyes, and in the briefest of moments, Sarah knew everything the girl was thinking. Whether she heard the thoughts flowing though Cora's mind or read the expression of her face, Sarah knew. And she thought Cora could probably say the same thing about her.

Whether or not this was really the way out of Cora's mind world, it was all they had. In the Clinic, a psychopathic killer was closing in on Cora. Who knew how close to her he was already? Whatever they were going to do, they had to do it now.

Anyway, she thought, *it's a win-win situation for Cora. If this jump kills her, at least she won't have to die at the hands of the man who murdered her family. And if this works, if this really is the way out . . . at least it would give her a fighting chance.* What it came down to was whether or not Sarah was willing to risk her life to save this girl. But that was a question she didn't even need to ask herself; she'd long since decided on an answer.

Sarah held her hand out and Cora took it. Her grip was tight, and Sarah could feel her shaking. She squeezed back reassuringly.

Together, they stepped to the edge of Alligator Rock. Below them, the water mist, bright in the light of the moon, swirled and billowed. Beyond it, hidden by all that whiteness, there might have been a tranquil pool or there might have been a rock-strewn riverbed. There was no way to tell.

Sarah squeezed Cora's hand once more; then without having to say one word, they stepped off the rock together.

Chapter 22

Sarah woke gasping for breath. Lungs burning, she grasped at her throat with both hands, as if her fingers could force air into her water-filled lungs. Her eyes were full of freezing cold water, and the world above her was bleary and out of focus. Someone was leaning over her, but she couldn't make out the face. Oh Jesus, she thought, I'm going to die. I'm really going to die.

"Come on, Sarah!" She heard Cole's voice yelling from what seemed like a great distance. "Breathe! Breathe, for Chrissake!"

Vaguely, she could feel Cole pressing her nostrils shut and blowing air into her mouth, but there was water in the air's way and it couldn't reach her lungs. She felt a hot tear fall from his eye onto the cold skin of her forehead and slide off.

She was incredibly conscious of what was going on inside her body. She could feel the water sloshing around in spaces meant to be hollow. There was water in her sinus cavities, and in her mouth.

Her peripheral vision was fading now, going black, as the lack of oxygen began to take a real toll on her body. Just a few more minutes and it would all be over. She felt so tired, like she could just let it happen . . . She could just give up and let herself drown in this bed. It wasn't even a matter of giving up. She was going to die, and there was nothing she could do to change that.

And it wasn't such a bad way to go, after all, much better than a car wreck or cancer, something painful. There was no pain here, just a gentle burn, a pressure in her lungs.

Now Cole was pinching her nostrils closed again, blowing air—

With a hitch and a loud retch, Sarah rolled onto her side and vomited up what must have been a gallon of cold water onto Cole's bedroom carpet. It kept coming and coming. She remembered throwing up like that once before, in the Emergency Room of a hospital after her graduation party at Duke. They'd pumped her stomach and drained almost a full quart of vodka from it. She remembered how her throat had felt in the morning. This was ten times worse.

She sucked in a breath, swallowing the air like it was Dom Perignon, then took another breath, and another, lying on her side, both arms thrown over her head. The air felt incredible going down her throat, so clean. Right then, the air in southern California probably would have tasted like pure oxygen.

Cole grabbed the blanket off his bed and wrapped it around her, then pulled her into an embrace.

"Thank God," he said, crying. "Oh, thank God, I thought you were going to—to—" He couldn't finish and broke down into a fit of sobbing. Though she felt unbelievably weak and wasn't trying, Sarah couldn't help picking up on the powerful signals Cole was giving off. All he was seeing right now was Jimmy. Jimmy dead by the pool, in the middle of all those people.

"Are you okay?" he said, when he'd gotten himself under some semblance of control. "What in the hell happened?"

"Cora," Sarah said, her voice no more than a strangled croak. It felt like someone had forced a balloon down her throat, and then, just for shits and giggles, started filling it with helium.

She pulled herself into a sitting position and propped her back up against the bed-frame, hugging the blanket tight around her freezing body. She was shivering so powerfully, she thought she might fly apart. "Cora pulled me into her mind. She needs help, Cole."

"What's wrong?" Wiping the last of the tears from his cheeks, Cole stood and grabbed a sweatshirt from his closet, then unfolded the blanket from around Sarah's bare shoulders and helped her put it on.

"The man who killed her family," Sarah said, starting to feel a little better. The worst of the shivering was fading and her throat wasn't as bad as she'd thought it was at first. "He's on the island."

"But that's impossible," Cole shot back, "her family was killed in Los Angeles."

"He's there."

Cole thought for a moment. "We have to get out there to her."

Sarah nodded and stood, swaying a little at first, then regaining her balance. She slipped on her jeans. "Do you know anyone with a boat?" she said.

Cole shook his head, then said, "But I think I know where we can find one."

They made the town's marina in no more than three minutes.

Cole brought his old Civic to a screeching halt, the front fender just feet from the chain-link fence surrounding the place.

"Hurry," he said, bursting from his seat and out of the car's door. Ripping his keys from the ignition, he moved quickly to the trunk and opened it, rooted around for a moment, and came up with a hammer. Nodding toward the fence, he said, "Let's go."

The gate Cole had pulled up in front of was at least ten feet tall, but the fence to either side of it was considerably shorter, and they both climbed up and over with ease. Cole led the way, holding Sarah's hand. Moving fast, they stayed low, running with knees and backs bent. There didn't appear to be anyone around, but the last thing they needed was for someone to spot them and call the police. Not when Cora's life was at stake.

Cole came to an abrupt halt behind a wooden building. Just ahead were the water line, and the docks. Perhaps ten different docks in all, each containing somewhere between five and ten slips. Sarah scanned her eyes over the boats, most of them trawlers, big hulks of wood and metal. Those were out of the question. They'd need a key to start them up.

"Ah," Cole said from beside her. "There." He was pointing to the dock farthest over to the right. A painted plaque hung at the foot of the gently swaying dock. The white letters read: SMUGGLER'S COVE. Tied to the dock's cleats was a small fleet of rental fishing boats, white and small, surely no bigger than rowboats, boasting outboard engines. No keys required.

Keeping their backs to the series of small cabins in which the marina kept their offices, Cole and Sarah made their way over to the rental boats.

"Shit," Sarah said as they approached the first of the boats. It was chained to the dock. So much for that idea.

She looked back in the direction they had come, scanning the rest of the boats for any potential candidates. The sound Cole's hammer made coming down on the padlock nearly gave her a massive coronary.

"Voila," he said, holding up the chain, now sans lock. "Strong chain, shitty lock. Will they never learn?"

"Impressive," Sarah responded. "Now for the hard part. You up for this?"

Cole surveyed the choppy water of the bay, looking out in the direction of the island. "Not much of a choice," he said. "Let's do this thing."

He helped Sarah into the boat, then climbed in himself and cast off. When they were a few feet from the dock, he gave the ripcord of the Evinrude a good yank and the engine roared into life with a puff of oily smoke.

Sitting down on the back bench with his back to the engine, Cole tucked the steering arm underneath his right arm and twisted the rubber throttle. The boat surged ahead, bow rising as the back of the boat dropped down.

Sitting in the bow of the little boat, Sarah looked back at Cole. He looked pale and shaky, but determined. It had been a hard night for both of them so far. God only knew how close she had been to death just a few minutes ago, but all she could think of now was how it must have felt for Cole to nearly have to bear witness to the death of his son all over again. It must have seemed like a waking nightmare, and now this, to be out here on the water in this tiny vessel . . .

Behind him, the lights of Stone Beach grew smaller and smaller until, a few minutes later, there was nothing but black.

Sarah turned back around toward the island. Far off, the lamp of the lighthouse on the island came around and flashed at them, then was gone again, sending its beam into the open ocean.

We're coming, Cora, Sarah thought, trying with all of her might to project the words toward the frightened little girl on the island. *We're coming, kiddo.*

She just hoped they wouldn't be too late, though something inside of her, a tight, clenching feeling passing back and forth between her mind and her stomach, was telling her that they already were.

Chapter 23

Cora had never been so cold in her life, not even when she was eight and fell through a patch of thin ice covering Lake Whitney, where her parents owned a cabin. Her father had pulled her out that day; he'd slithered his way out to the hole on his belly and pulled her free of the icy water, then carried her all the way back to the cabin, more than a mile away, whispering, "It's all right, baby, it's going to be all right," into her ear the whole time, one warm hand on the freezing skin of her back, stroking, stroking. She wished he were here now. She needed him so badly . . .

For the first few minutes after waking up in her bed at the Clinic, beneath sheets sopping wet with frigid water, she'd felt as though the shivers running through her body would break her into pieces. Even her insides had quaked, her stomach and organs jumping and twitching as though electrified. Now, what felt like hours later, the worst of the shivering had passed, but the chill in her flesh had only intensified, gradually developing into a nearly complete physical numbness. She was aware of her feet and hands, but couldn't actually feel them at the ends of her legs and arms. There was a dull pain, though, from where she thought her hands and feet should be; she hoped that meant they were still there.

Adding to her plight was an intense psychological disorientation. Running from the madman in her mental version of

Bridgewater, she'd just assumed that when she woke up she'd be as good as new, able to get up and resume her life. But she wasn't. Upon first opening her eyes, she'd been horrified by what she saw, not because she felt immediately threatened by the dark room around her, but because what she could see made no sense. Her mind was still looking for the reality of the place where she'd secluded herself for the past weeks, and was having difficulty reacclimating itself to the real world. Her mind had become more keenly honed than ever during her stay in Bridgewater, but her senses, the ones with which her brain interpreted the physical world, had suffered, atrophied. Like any muscles, getting them back to full strength was going to take time. But time was one more thing Cora didn't have.

So focused had she been on her reawakening process that she had somehow managed to completely forget the madman who was stalking her. Suddenly it slammed into her that he was here. Here! Instinctively, she reached out for him, probing with the powerful fingers of her brain. It didn't take long to find him.

Sleeping. He was sleeping. Maybe she still had a chance. If only she could move . . .

With a monumental effort, Cora turned her head to the side and scanned the darkness. She made out the perimeter of what she thought was a machine. It was big and partially blocked her view of the door, which she could see part of, its perimeter outlined by the slightly brighter hallway beyond. Turning her head the other way, she made out the forms of the EKG and EEG monitors. They made a steady, soft sound, intertwining with each other in a way that was somehow soothing and almost musical. Beyond the monitors, a window, but no stars. And something falling. Snow. The flakes were lit brilliantly white for a moment as a light passed over them. But then the light was gone and Cora wondered if she'd ever seen it at all.

Move a voice scolded her from inside. *Run! He could be coming!*

But Cora was suddenly very tired, exhausted, in fact. She didn't think she'd ever been as tired in her whole life. *No,* she thought, *he's not coming, he's asleep. I have time to rest for a minute.*

It took every ounce of resolve she had not to let her eyes drift closed.

On either side of the bed she lay in, bars had been set in place to keep her from rolling off. She'd seen bars like these when she went to visit her friend Charise in the hospital after she'd broken her leg playing field hockey. All you had to do to lower them was pull up, and then they'd swing away. *All you had to do.* The phrase seemed ridiculous to Cora now, torturous.

I can do this, Cora thought, *I can. I have to.* She closed her eyes and took a breath, then another, filling her lungs with all the air she could, trying to prime her muscles. Then she opened her eyes, focused on the rails on the left side of the bed, and with a grunt of monumental effort lifted her left hand toward them.

Her hand got about halfway there before falling back to the bed, palm-up, like a tired spider.

"No," Cora said, and tried to lift the hand again, but all she managed to do was to push it across the white sheet toward the edge of the bed. This time she couldn't even achieve lift-off. "Please," she tried to say, but all that came out was a groan of pure hopelessness and misery. There was no way, no way . . . she was going to die. Whether the killer remained sleeping for five minutes or five hours, she'd still be here when he got to her. She may as well have been locked in a jail cell.

And that was when the first wave of anger passed over her. Whether it was directed at the killer or at the world in general, she didn't know, or care. All she cared about was not being helpless anymore, not being trapped anymore. For too long she'd been forced by fate to play the role of victim; she'd lost her mother and father and little brother, and now, after all of that, after living when she should have died as well, it was going to end here, with her, still helpless, in this bed.

Blood was pounding in her head so hard she felt faint with it, but it was now or never.

One more time she raised her hand toward the bars. *Just for a second,* she thought, *I can do it, I can . . .* Straining, eyes rolling back in her head, pushing up, using her elbow to gain leverage on the mattress, Cora felt the tips of her fingers graze the bottom bar. Hope blossomed in her chest. If she could just reach it, hold onto it . . . *come on.* But her arm was starting to shake; she could feel the strength running out of it, ebbing fast. A horrible whining sound escaped her mouth, growing with intensity as her fingers dropped lower and lower, becoming a full scream as her hand settled back down on the mattress, trembled, and then was still. But the scream continued, dying down only when Cora ran out of breath and lay, panting, vision clouded red and staticky.

When she opened her eyes again, she didn't trust what they told her she was seeing.

The bars on the left side of the bed were gone. *What the hell?* There was no way she'd gotten enough into her push, was there? She thought she'd only just grazed the bars.

And there was a funny smell in the air. *No,* she corrected herself, *that's not a smell, it's a taste.* But it was more like both. With a dry tongue, Cora licked her upper lip and tasted blood, salty and metallic. The smell was like old pennies.

The blood was from her nose, and it was really coming

now, hot and steady, not a trickle, but a stream. She could feel it running down over lips and dripping from her chin onto her chest. And there was a pain in her head, too, sharp and dull at once, stabbing in front and throbbing deeper.

The bleeding worried Cora, but it was already starting to taper off a little bit, as was the worst of the pain in her head.

Dropping her weight into one shoulder and then the other, she began to rock herself from side to side, also trying to get her hips and torso into the routine. With one last push, throwing every ounce of strength she could into her neck and shoulders, Cora went over.

She hit the floor hard, but the floor wasn't the first thing she hit. On the way down, something sharp gashed her upper leg, bringing a fresh wave of agony, but only until it was replaced by the pain of her impact with the unforgiving floor.

She hit face first, her left cheek and shoulder taking the brunt of it. Her legs reached the floor a fraction of a second later. The kneecap of her right leg hit the floor square, and Cora felt the jolt run up through her leg and into her right side, where it settled like a toothache just below her shoulder.

Stunned, Cora lay on her left side, legs twisted at the hips, right knee on the floor. Finally, she remembered to breathe, and drew in a long, quavering lungful of air. Her eyes were watering, and the flow of blood from her nose had regained some vigor. She could feel it trickling hot and fast down her cheek.

She rolled onto her back, where she lay, trying to catch her breath.

The pain was coming from everywhere now: her head, arms, legs. The good side of it was that Cora could at least feel those places now.

Looking back up at the bed, she was shocked by what she saw for the second time in just a few moments.

The railing which had been in place along the left side of the bed, the one she thought she'd managed to disengage, was gone, but not because it'd fallen down and away, as it was meant to.

The railing was torn and twisted, stainless steel twisted back toward both the foot and head of the bed. The railing hadn't been disengaged at all; it was blown out as though a high-powered explosive had been detonated in the center of it. Only an explosive which hadn't affected anything but the railing.

It was a segment of the torn railing that had ripped Cora's leg as she fell, leaving a long but shallow gash on her quadriceps.

I did that, Cora thought, staring at the ruined railing. *Somehow I did that.* The thought invigorated and terrified her at once. It wasn't the first time she'd affected an object close to her, but in the past she'd never managed anything more extraordinary than rolling a pencil off the edge of a table, and even that had been unintentional. Nothing like this. Never. Something had changed.

Straining, Cora rolled back over onto her stomach, pushing the thought from her mind.

The way she'd landed, her head was in the direction of the room's door.

Using her elbows and upper arms to propel herself, she pushed in that direction, straining with her feet also. She was regaining some strength and wind, and surprised herself with the relative speed at which she was able to move.

Having arrived at the door, Cora used the wall to pull herself into a sitting position, then reached up to try the knob. It didn't budge. Locked.

Exhausted again, Cora let out a sob and leaned her head back against the wall.

Chapter 24

It was the rats that woke him.

Luis bolted to his feet in the darkness, shedding the blanket, which was heavy with furry bodies.

They were moving all over him, on his neck, his legs, his stomach, biting him, clawing him. He shook himself like a dog drying itself, felt the rats fly off him like water, heard them land squealing, skid across the cement floor, scrabble to their clawed feet, and come back for him.

Light!

Luis fell to his knees and groped over the floor for the penlight, pushing through the rats, feeling their warm little bodies pulsating beneath his fingers. Jesus, there must be thousands of them. The sound in the room was intolerably loud, a cacophony of squeaks and squeals and shrieks.

A rat sunk its teeth into the skin of his knuckle and he screamed and shook his hand, sending the filthy animal flying off somewhere. He put his hands back down, feeling more rats crawling over the backs of his legs, on his back, in his hair.

There!

He snapped on the light and shook himself again, and heard bodies whap heavily into the walls and onto the floor.

"Get off me!" he screamed. "Get the fuck off!"

He twisted the head of the penlight and the room was revealed, squirming, writhing. The floor was a shifting sea of brown and gray bodies. The rats crawled over each other, swarming toward him, fighting one another for the prize meal, him.

A door.

Luis spotted the black square in the wall and bolted for it.

Under his feet, the bones of rats crunched and snapped. He stomped down harder, almost gleefully, crushing skulls and backs, turning the rats into spongy paste beneath the heels of his boots.

And then he was out, into a hallway with rough-hewn stone walls dark with wetness, moving fast, still shaking his arms and legs, making sure none of the dirty scavengers remained affixed to him to rip and bite him.

He stopped, panting and sweating, when he realized they were gone. The rats had bitten him in dozens of places on his hands and legs and back, and the skin in those places felt fiery, every single nerve ending alive and howling in agony. God only knew what diseases the rats could be carrying. The thought made Luis shudder in revulsion and he wished he had a place to clean the bite wounds, to get the germs out of his flesh before they infected him and made him sick.

A powerful sound snapped Luis from his thoughts. Not a loud sound, really, but a strong one, from far off, but still audible. And he could feel it, too. A throaty rumble. It vibrated in his feet.

Luis listened, turning his ear one way down the hall, and then the other, trying to figure out which direction the sound was coming from. It seemed as though it was coming from all around him, from the walls and floor and ceiling.

He shone the light back the way he had come and saw the door to the rat-room in the distance, gaping blackly like an open mouth. He couldn't tell if the squeaks and cries he heard coming from the room were real or imagined. Either way, there was no way in hell he was going back through that room.

His mind made up, Luis headed the other way down the long hall, walking fast, trying to keep the cold at bay, feeling with every passing second another place where he'd been bitten or scratched. He passed door after door, some closed, some open, leading into darkened rooms filled with the barely discernable shapes of chairs and tables and desks.

He wondered what this place was that he'd crawled into, this deserted, tomb-like maze. It almost felt as though he'd been sealed inside some kind of complex mausoleum, or maybe an Egyptian pyramid, and now, after thousands of years of sleep with the rats and the dankness of old air, he'd woken to walk the world again.

The sound of dripping water was all around, overlapping layers of auditory impulse, nearby and far-off, not loud, but deafening at the same time. The rhythm of it was hypnotic, soothing.

A serene certainty quickly overtook him, a single-minded purposefulness. The pain of his wounds faded into the background, where he could still feel them in some distant way, but where they didn't distract him.

With no forethought whatsoever, Luis stopped and walked through the door on his right, shining the little penlight on the ground a few feet in front of him.

The door led to another hall, almost exactly like the one he'd just exited. Luis headed quickly down it, strides long and confident, thoughtless.

The floor was a half-inch thick in dust, and his feet kicked it up in thick, brown clouds as he moved. At the end of the hall were three identical doors. Luis took the one on the left, knowing even before he opened it that the door would open into a stairwell. He took the stairs up, ascending them two at a time.

The stairs went up only one level and, as Luis passed through the door at the top, he saw a giant, red LEVEL 3 painted on the wall.

This hall was different. Gone were the stone walls and the dampness. Even the sound of water dripping was distant and faint, coming from below now.

The walls of this new hall were made of cinder block, painted white, though the paint had chipped badly and was almost entirely gone. The hall's ceiling had been done in tile, with panels of fluorescent lights at intervals, but almost all of the tiles had fallen to the floor and rotted into piles of dust and plastic, and several of the long, fluorescent tube-shaped light bulbs had detached from their sockets and dangled by wires, like snakes from tree-branches.

Luis made his way down the dusty hall, pushing the dangling bulbs out of his way with the hand not occupied with the penlight. He could hear them swinging back and forth behind him and had the urge to turn and make sure they weren't coiling to strike at him.

The strange sense of calm which had taken him so suddenly was gone, and had been replaced by a sense that he was supposed to know what to do from here, that he should know, but didn't. He was missing something.

He stopped and stood still, holding his breath, listening. The rumbling sound he'd heard before was closer, more powerful, definitely coming from somewhere in front of him. And now, for the first time, Luis noted the warmth of the air, so much less cold here than one level down.

It struck him suddenly what the rumbling sound was. A furnace.

Grinning, Luis strode to the one door at the end of the hall and opened it. A pleasant wave of heat rolled into him, warming his chilled flesh.

Following the sound of the roaring furnace, now so loud he could hear nothing else, Luis took turn after turn, and in minutes stood inside the sweltering boiler-room.

There were footprints in the dust all over the place here, especially around the furnace itself, which likely required pretty frequent maintenance to keep it running smoothly. It was an old furnace, a real monster, tubes and pipes and ducts all over the place.

One door besides the one he'd entered led out of the room, and Luis headed for it, already dripping with sweat though he'd been in the room only seconds, feeling strange from the enormous swing in body temperature he'd experienced over the past few minutes.

Something caught his eye, and he turned to it.

On the wall to his right, there was a large, gray metal box. Silver metallic cords trailed down the cinderblock wall and led into it from above. From above where the girl was. The fuse box.

The door of the box stood slightly ajar, and now Luis pulled it open the rest of the way, revealing two long, vertical rows of black switches, each tagged with a white label. The labels were marked in thin black pen, with ROOM 1 all the way through ROOM 38, and there were several more which appeared to have nothing to do with the building itself, things like BOATHOUSE LIGHTS and LIGHTHOUSE.

Using the flat of his hand, Luis began switching all the breaker switches from ON to OFF. They flipped to OFF with a satisfying snapping sound, hearty, like finger-bones breaking.

Beyond the door, Luis found more stairs, leading up.

He played his flashlight over the door at the top of the

stairs and held his breath, zoning out everything else but the throbbing beacon in the front of his skull.

Up there, he thought, sliding his fingers over the razor in his pocket, tracing the smoothness of the long groove between the handle and the back of the folded blade with an almost sexual awareness. *That little bitch is right up there, that little bitch . . . I want my life back.*

With a grimace on his face that might have been a smile, Luis started up the stairs.

Chapter 25

The beam of the lighthouse came around, momentarily bathing the boat and its two occupants in light, and then it was gone again, painting a long oval on the smooth water to their left, leaving Cole and Sarah alone in the dark, dark night.

Sarah looked up and wasn't surprised to see that there was no moon tonight. No stars, either. It was as deep a night as she could remember.

Dropping her eyes back down, Sarah saw that they were getting close now, close enough for her to be able to see the lights in the office of the Clinic, high atop the island's lone hill. Maybe two or three hundred more yards.

"Look," she yelled, glancing back at Cole over her shoulder, pointing toward the island. "Almost there!" Because she thought he could use it, she flashed him the best smile she could muster. Not much, but something.

Cole nodded and gave her a quick thumbs-up, easier than yelling back into the wind. He held his body rigidly, and with every rock of the boat Sarah saw him tense as if the craft were about to go over, leaning to the rising side with all his weight. *All in all,* she thought, *it was a pretty safe bet to guess he'd rather be elsewhere.*

Suddenly the lights of the Clinic were gone, and only blackness lay in front of them.

"What the hell?" she said, squinting into the night, hoping

that her view of the Clinic was just being obscured by trees. *But what about the lighthouse, then?* she thought. *It's out, too.*

Behind her, Cole was yelling something. She turned to see what he wanted and found that he had one arm stretched out toward her, holding a flashlight.

"Here!" he yelled. "I found it under my seat!"

Sarah pressed the rubber button just below the wide head of the flashlight and a strong beam appeared. Ah, she thought, that's better.

She turned back toward the island and panned the beam over the water. The flashlight was powerful, and in the distance Sarah could see the vertical black lines of tree trunks.

There was a bump from below and something scraped along the boat's hull and then was gone.

"What the hell was that?" Cole yelled.

Sarah shone the light down at the water in front of them. She saw the huge rock almost in time.

Cole saw it at the same moment and tried to cut the throttle and turn, but it was too late and the lightweight fishing boat rode up the side of the rock, teetered for a moment on its side like a car doing a wheelie in an episode of the "Dukes of Hazzard," then went over, spilling Cole and Sarah headfirst into the water.

Sarah hit the water curled into fetal position, which was fortunate, because if she'd splashed down uncurled, her head would have been cracked open on a sharply jutting column of stone, like an egg on the lip of a bowl.

Cole, on the other hand, hit the water face first, driving his left shoulder directly into a submerged ridge of rock. With an unbelievable burst of pain, Cole felt his collarbone break and his shoulder dislocate, and, what was maybe the worst part of it, he heard the bones giving way with the groaning reluctance of green wood bent over a knee.

The slab of stone Cole had crashed into was long and wide and ran like a table just six inches or so beneath the surface of the bay. He lay there on his back, seemingly atop the water, writhing in agony, wanting to scream but unable to get the sound out. It was stuck somewhere below his throat and above his chest, caged there by his clenched muscles.

Sarah waded over to him. The water was shallow here, and came up only halfway between her waist and her shoulders. It was incredibly cold, though, and she knew that if they didn't get out of the bay soon, they'd begin the painful and inevitable progression into hypothermia.

"Cole," she said. There was blood on his shirt, and for a second Sarah was afraid his clavicle had splintered and torn through the skin of his shoulder, but when she moved his shirt aside, she saw that the shoulder was just badly abraded. No bone stuck through. "Thank God," she said. "Cole, can you walk? We have to get to shore."

She saw him fighting to get control of himself. He took a long, slow breath and then blew it out, and then fixed on her eyes and nodded.

Carefully, she slipped her hands underneath his back and lifted, helping him to sit. Cautious though she was, it was impossible to spare the shoulder completely, and he hissed in renewed pain. Sitting up now, she could see the damage more clearly. His left shoulder hung far below the right. If he'd been doing it for fun, in mockery of Quasimodo or Mr. Hyde, it would have been humorous, but considering the circumstances, it was horrible.

Holding her hand out for him, she helped Cole stand, and they started toward shore, wading slowly.

The flashlight, apparently of the water-resistant variety, bobbed in the water just a few feet away, head facing up, lending its beam to the sky. Sarah left Cole's side for just long enough to snatch it out of the cold water, then returned quickly to him. He draped his good arm again around her shoulders, and she wrapped her arm tight about his waist.

Wading through the chest-high water was difficult, but Sarah realized the boon the high water level had been only when they began to near shore and the level started dropping. All of a sudden, Cole and Sarah were made victim to their tired bodies, wet clothes, and gravity, which threatened to pull them to the ground.

Sarah searched the darkness ahead, but there was still no sign of the Clinic's lights.

"Don't putz out on me now, Cole," she said, trying to keep her tone flip. "We've still got a job to do here." The adrenaline in her system had begun to wear off and Sarah was getting a nasty case of the shivers. Cole was even worse. He was like a human jackhammer beside her, and when she looked over at him, she could see how pale he was, his face a splotch of white in the dark. Shock, she thought, he's going into shock. If she didn't get him somewhere warm soon, this was going to get ugly.

And Sarah wasn't feeling so great herself. She was starting to feel euphoric and lightheaded and knew full-blown hypothermia couldn't be far off. "Hurry," she said through lips she couldn't feel.

They moved toward the shore of the bay, slipping time after time on submerged rocks and seaweed. It seemed like they would never reach dry ground. Each time the water started to get shallower, it would drop off again, and Sarah and Cole would find themselves up to their necks in the frigid water. It was only when Sarah was really beginning to doubt her ability to continue on that the water level finally dropped for good. Stumbling like a pair of drunks, Cole's weight more than ever resting on Sarah's burning shoulders, they emerged from the water and lurched toward the line of trees, that Sarah could make out only faintly in the scant light.

And then, somehow, the trees were behind them and the Clinic was in front of them, dark and hulking, windows lightless, like a dead person's eyes. But Sarah knew there was life inside this old husk.

When they reached the door to the Clinic, Cole said, "The keys, my front pocket." With a hand she was able to feel less and less with every second that passed, Sarah retrieved Cole's keys from his front pants pocket. Cole took them from her and, after scraping the key over the lock several times, fitted it in and twisted it. Sarah yanked the door open and they both nearly toppled inside.

"The office," Cole said, panting, sweat pouring off his forehead despite the cold. As they made their way up the hall, Sarah stripped off the sweatshirt she wore and let the sopping garment splat to the floor.

They reached the office and Sarah carried Cole to the duty desk and propped him up against it. Cole was still conscious, but barely, his eyes glazed and distant. He was literally as white as snow, the only color in his face the blue irises of his eyes. Even his lips were pale, barely distinguishable from the rest of his face.

Blankets, Sarah thought. In the rear portion of the office, there were several gray metallic cabinets. Sarah moved quickly to the first in line and pulled open the door. The shelves were stocked with first-aid supplies. Sarah snatched the two widest Ace bandages she could find, then opened the next of the metal cabinets. It was filled with sheets and blankets. Sarah grabbed two of the brown institutional blankets and then returned to Cole's side.

She stripped off her T-shirt and pants and wrapped one of the blankets around her shoulders. It was warm against her skin, which was now starting to burn from the heat of the place. The temperature difference between the water of the bay and the inside of the Clinic must have been at least thirty or forty degrees.

"Help me get these off you," she said to Cole, unbuttoning his jeans and yanking them down. He sat back on the edge of the desk and raised his legs as best he could, letting Sarah slip first his shoes and socks and then the wet jeans off. When she was done with that, she turned her attention to his button-down and T-shirt. There was no way she was going to be able to pull the T-shirt over his head without causing him an immense amount of pain, but she needed to get at that shoulder.

Moving around to the front of the desk, she pulled the middle drawer open. There was clutter inside, papers and Post-It notes and pens and pencils all in a jumble. Sarah rooted through with both hands, slid her hands underneath, feeling along the wooden bottom of the drawer. *Ah-ha!* She pulled the scissors out and returned to Cole.

"Snip-snip," he said, swaying dreamily. The look in his eyes was dazed and vacant.

Working quickly and efficiently, Sarah sliced Cole's flannel shirt up the sleeve and then snipped the collar, then repeated the process on the other side. Cole's T-shirt was next.

"That was my favorite shirt," Cole mumbled. "You'll pay." He smiled wanly.

Standing back, Sarah got her first good look at Cole's shoulder.

"Oh, man," she said under her breath. The skin was stretched tight where the joint of the shoulder had come unhinged. The whole area was discolored and purplish. It didn't even look like a human arm anymore.

"Cole," she said, "have you ever dislocated your shoulder before?"

Cole's head was drooping, his chin making a slow journey to his chest. Sarah slapped him lightly on the cheek and he raised it again.

"Ever dislocated your shoulder before?"

Cole nodded, two drugged lurches of his head. "Football," he said, "senior year of high school."

"Good," Sarah said. "Then you know how much this is going to hurt."

Cole nodded again, then said one word. "Fuck."

Sarah bent down and reached into the back pocket of Cole's jeans. She pulled out his wallet, which was thin and leather.

"Open your mouth," she said to Cole and, when he did, she stuck the wallet between Cole's teeth. "Bite down if you have to."

With no further warning, Sarah placed one hand on Cole's ruined shoulder and grabbed his arm at the elbow with the other, then yanked down hard. With one quick shove, she guided the bone back into its socket and then released Cole's shoulder again.

Cole made a strange squealing noise and opened his mouth, releasing the wallet. It fell to the floor, and Sarah could see the deep tooth-marks in the leather. "Oh, thank God," Cole said, sucking in a deep breath.

Sarah picked up one of the Ace bandages from the desk and wrapped it tightly around Cole's shoulder, looping it a couple of times around his ribs, hoping it would help to keep the bone in its socket. When she'd finished, she took the second bandage and used it to secure Cole's arm against his body, forearm pressed against his chest.

Sarah then draped the remaining blanket over his shoulders. As she did, Cole said, "Cora."

"I know," Sarah answered, "I know."

Hanging on the back of the swivel chair at the desk was a brown cardigan. Sarah put it on, the wool scratchy against her arms and back, but warm.

"Look in the cabinet on the left," Cole said, "top shelf."

Moving fast, Cora on her mind, Sarah returned to the metal cabinets and pulled open the door of the only cabinet she hadn't looked inside yet.

It was full of boxes, most of which were sealed with clear tape and marked with the names of medical supply companies. A large one on the top shelf, however, was open, and something green, it looked like a sleeve, hung over the side. Sarah reached up on her tiptoes and pulled the big box down, then looked inside. It was full of clothes, most of which looked old and a little mildewy. The odor coming up from the clothes confirmed it.

Sarah carried the box over to Cole and sorted through the box until she found them each a pair of sweatpants. She also pulled out an oversized green sweatshirt for Cole and helped him get it over his head, tucking the empty arm inside the sweatshirt to keep it from swinging.

"What is this stuff, anyway?" she asked as she was pulling on the pair of sweatpants she'd chosen for herself. They were blue and far too big, and sported the emblem of the New England Patriots.

"Most of it's the stuff patients were wearing when they came in," Cole answered. "Sweats are real popular with the families of catatonics. Easy on, easy off."

Neither of them wore shoes or socks, but the overall improvement was immense. Sarah had stopped shivering altogether, and some of the color was returning to Cole's face.

"You ready?" Sarah asked.

"Let's go," he said, pushing away from the edge of the desk.

Chapter 26

Luis stopped in front of the girl's door, still wiping blood from his razor with the bottom of his shirt.

When he had opened the door at the top of the stairs leading up from the basement, he'd found himself almost face to face with a woman in a white nurse's uniform. She'd been coming out of a room directly across the hall, and before she could scream or run, Luis had driven her backward through the still-open door and then finished her with his razor. It was a pleasureless killing, though. He'd had other things on his mind, and as soon as the nurse had breathed her sputtering last, Luis had been off again in search of the girl. It hadn't taken long.

From beyond the door he could feel her, so close now, practically begging to be cut. His life back. So soon now. He wondered what it would feel like; if she would disappear from his brain in a flash, or if it would be more like a gradual dwindling away. He wondered how he should kill her, and if that would matter. So many delicious questions to be answered.

He reached out and turned the knob, but the door was locked.

Luis stepped back and then, with a grunt, slammed the bottom of his foot into the door, just below the knob. Once. Twice.

The kicks sounded loud and hollow in the hall, but the door didn't so much as quiver. It was solid metal. His foot hadn't even left a dent. He wasn't going to get anywhere like this, not even if he stood here and pounded on the door for three hours.

He stood back from the door and looked down the hall to his left, searching for anything he might use to break the door down, but there was nothing, just a dark and empty hall.

He'd have to use his gun, something he'd not wanted to do. Every gun leaves a unique series of marks on a fired bullet, like a fingerprint on a human being. That was how ballistics experts were so often able to trace a round to the type of gun it was fired from, and, quite often, even to the exact gun from which it had been fired. Not the kind of evidence Luis wanted to leave behind.

Slicing some old fuck to pieces with his razor was one thing, but using his gun was quite another. That was risky; he'd already been stupid once today, using the gun to off the dog when he'd stolen the boat.

Switching the razor to his left hand and drawing his Glock 17, Luis comforted himself with the knowledge that firing the gun point-blank into a steel door would almost certainly mash the bullet so badly that no ID could be made, other than that the weapon it had been fired from was a 9 millimeter handgun of some sort. Metal did things to bullets that human flesh didn't. Anyway, he'd be using the razor on the girl.

He stepped back a few feet from the door and drew a bead on the doorknob, then squeezed the trigger.

The report was deafening in the hall, less a bang than a steely KLING, like a sledgehammer coming down hard on an anvil. There was the same ringing reverberation in Luis's ears afterwards, and he wished he'd thought to cover them with something before firing.

A small, round hole no larger than a dime had appeared just to the right of the doorknob: a perfect shot. Luis hoped that the girl hadn't been injured by a fragment of flying shrapnel. It would be a real shame if she were already in pain before he'd even started with her.

He reached out with a foot and nudged the door with his toe. It swung open silently, revealing darkness beyond. Luis reholstered the Glock and moved the razor back to his right hand, holding it easy and loose.

Stepping forward, Luis saw something he couldn't immediately identify. Two lines of light, one green and one blue, seemed to float in mid-air, one directly above the other. As he moved closer, though, two things happened which allowed him to gain understanding. The first was that the ringing in his ears the gunshot had caused was gradually dying off, and was replaced instead by a high-pitched whining sound, an incessant EEEEEEEEEEEEEE—

At the same time, his eyes were becoming accustomed to the lack of light, and he saw the gray outlines of the monitors which were producing the blue and green lines. He immediately understood. An EEG and EKG. It wasn't so long ago that his own mother had spent her last days hooked up to those same machines. This was a medical facility of some sort. He wondered if the girl had been injured somehow.

Just beneath the monitors, there was a bed, but his view of it was blocked by a big machine and an IV drip mounted atop a thin, metal pole. A roll of paper was affixed to the back of the machine, and as Luis watched, a thin needle scrawled a flat line over an otherwise blank sheet.

Luis raised the razor and stepped around the machine.

Even as he did, though, he knew something was wrong. It should have felt different, closing in on the girl like this; it should have felt certain, but instead it felt anti-climactic, no different than he'd felt standing outside of her door. He knew what he would see even before he did.

The bed was empty.

"No!" he growled and slashed down at the mattress, gashing it deeply. "Where are you?" He spun around and searched the small room for any sign of her, but there was nothing. "Cunt," he said. "Bitch." He could feel insanity pressing him. It was solid around him, like the air. He was wading through it. With a snarl, he lashed out with a foot and kicked the table that supported the monitors. It rocketed backward and slammed into the far wall of the room. One of the monitors, jarred into violent movement by the impact, flew off the table and smashed into the room's sole window, cracking the glass in a spider web pattern before dropping with a loud crunch to the floor. Unable to stop himself, Luis turned his rage toward the big machine in front of the bed, toppling it over with one hard push. It landed with a crash, and glass and plastic flew in every direction. There was a bright flash as something inside the machine shorted out, and then a loud grinding sound, and then only silence, save for a soft fizzling sound as the big machine's guts began to burn.

This couldn't be happening! She was here somewhere. Inside his mind, he could still feel her. Close by. But where?

There was a sound and Luis stopped, freezing where he stood like a marble statue, hands just inches from the IV tree, which he'd been intending to hurl against the wall.

It came again, hollow, and somehow close by while sounding distant at the same time. Percussive almost, like a deep drumbeat. *What the hell?*

Luis dropped to his knees and ripped aside the white sheet hanging off the side of the hospital bed, but the girl wasn't underneath.

He stood and surveyed the wrecked room.

In the corner stood a cream-colored metal locker. Luis strode quickly to it and yanked the door open. Inside, there hung several shirts and dresses. Luis batted them aside with a hand, making sure the girl wasn't crouched down behind, though already he knew she wasn't.

It was when he turned back around, anxiously fingering the blade of the razor, that he saw the duct grate resting flat on the floor. He hadn't seen it before, because the bed had blocked his view.

The sound came again, and now Luis understood it. He rushed over the duct and slid to a stop on his knees in front of it, directing the beam of the flashlight inside.

The duct was perhaps two feet wide and a foot and a half high, if that. After about ten yards, the duct sloped downward, and Luis could see only the gray metal walls of the duct in the light. A draft of warm air lightly buffeted his face as he looked down the narrow duct.

Down, he thought, *the ducts go down*. But of course they did.

Luis stood and there was a feral smile on his face. The ducts went down because that's where the heat came from; down was where the furnace was.

His prior rage forgotten, Luis headed out of the room and back down the hall the way he'd come, breaking into a slow jog.

Chapter 27

Raising her hand one more time, Cora brought her fist down on the grate and it swung away with a squeak and a bang. She curled her fingers around the edge of the hole in front of her and pulled herself forward, groaning at the excruciating pain in her arms.

She peered down into the room below.

In the dim light thrown by the furnace, Cora could just barely make out the floor, maybe ten or twelve feet below her. A long drop, but she didn't have much choice in the matter. It was either through the opening or cook in the duct, which at this distance from the furnace was almost unbearably hot.

Positioning herself directly over the hole, her hands on one side and her knees on the other, Cora tried to slide her legs through first so she could hold on with her arms and hang before she dropped, minimizing the distance of the fall.

She got one leg through and was reaching for a seam in the metal of the duct when her other leg abruptly slid through the hole, leaving her dangling from the opening by her arms alone.

Her sweaty fingers slipped over the metal as she hung seven feet above the ground, searching for some kind of purchase on the floor of the duct. Whimpering, she clawed for any kind of support, but there was nothing. She let out a small cry as her hands slid to the edge of the hole.

She dangled for a brief moment from her fingertips. And then she was falling.

Cora hit the cement floor awkwardly, landing half on and half off of a short wooden footstool, her right leg twisted back beneath her body, yanking the knee in a direction it wasn't supposed to bend.

The pain was extraordinary. For a moment the room was bright red. Some rational part of her tried impossibly hard to stop the scream from coming, knowing that it would only serve to inform the killer of her location, but it would not be denied and came free with a throat-rasping ferocity.

Breathless and crying, Cora hauled herself into a sitting position, feeling bones grinding together in her knee and hip. As slowly as she could, she pulled the leg out from underneath herself, moving it with one of her hands while she propped herself up with the other.

Keep it together, she thought, blinking back tears. She took several deep breaths, holding each one and then expelling it slowly, trying her best to compartmentalize the pain, to stow it someplace where it couldn't hurt her, something she'd learned from her soccer coach the year before, while playing through the pain of a severely sprained ankle.

It didn't do much for the pain itself this time; Cora thought there was likely something broken in her leg, if not more than one thing. But the exercise in concentration did allow her overwhelmed mind to calm itself, to push to the forefront of her brain the important thing, and that was staying alive. Pain was one thing; dying at the hands of a psychotic killer was another altogether.

Cora surveyed the room around her. At least she surveyed what little she could see in the light provided by the two yellow-orange pilot lights of the big furnace.

There appeared to be two doors out of the room, one

leading up a flight of stairs, that one to the Clinic, Cora assumed, and one leading deeper into the darkness. The latter was on the side of the room closer to where she had fallen.

That one, she thought, looking at the second door; I need to go there. He'll be coming for me down those stairs any second.

But even as she started in the direction of the far door, pulling herself over the dirty floor with her hands and one good leg, she began to question the wisdom of her choice.

What good would it do to run? Not that she'd have been up for a marathon before her fall from the heating duct, but now, with one leg all but useless, the very idea of fleeing seemed almost laughable.

I could hide, she thought. But she quickly dismissed that idea.

First off, the killer probably had a flashlight, and anywhere she managed to secret herself away, he'd be able to see her. Not to mention the fact that he'd been drawn to her from all the way across the country. She didn't think the homing beacon in his own head was going to fail him now, not when he was so close.

As it turned out, the decision was made for her.

There was a loud bang from the top of the staircase and bright light filtered into the boiler room, jostling wildly as the person who wielded the flashlight descended the stairs.

Cora was suddenly incapacitated—not by fear, but by a vision.

No longer was she in her own body, but in his, a passenger in his mind, seeing through his eyes.

He took the stairs two at a time, murderous glee singing in his veins. Through his eyes, she saw the beam of light flooding over the stairs, over the floor of the boiler room. She saw the footstool she'd fallen on. It was striped red, white, and blue with stars, like the American flag.

And his thoughts were hers to hear, as well: what he was thinking, what he was feeling.

Mostly, what she felt was anticipation. The anticipation of the cutting.

Upstairs, he had been denied, but he could feel her now, still pulling him in, like a piece of metal drawn to a magnet, just feet away, and he would soon have what he'd come all this long way for. Peace.

At the bottom of the stairs the killer stopped and directed the light into the room, breathing heavily, not from exertion, but from excitement.

She saw herself.

Sitting on the other side of the room with her dirty legs and arms, what she looked most like to herself was a child who'd taken a bad fall during recess on the playground. But this child was wearing a hospital gown, torn at one shoulder, and one of her knees was puffed to twice the size it should have been. There was blood on her elbows, chin, and both knees. There was also a dribble of red from one temple.

Abruptly, the manic craze for cutting she'd felt before lessened, and it was partially replaced by something decidedly different, something terrifying.

Cora felt the killer's eyes return to the rip in her gown, to the shoulder the gown hung off of, revealing just the tiniest bit of curve . . . and then his eyes traveled down, down to her legs, spread out in front of her, and up to the place where her gown had bunched up around her thighs, to the shadowy darkness there.

Just as quickly as it had come upon her, the vision ended and Cora snapped back into her own body, horrified at what she had felt in his mind, at what he meant to do before he finished her.

He was shining the light directly into her eyes, and she couldn't see him.

Blindly, not wanting to take her eyes off the light because it gave her some idea of where he was, Cora began retreating toward the door she'd seen, moving as quickly as she could.

The killer stood his ground, not following her, just watching.

Just as she reached the doorway, he spoke. Slowly, he began walking toward her. Cora could hear his shoes crunching dust and grit underfoot.

"I've come a long way for this, bitch," he said quietly, almost conversationally, "a long way."

Cora backed through the doorway and into the hall beyond. When she was through, she kicked the door with her good leg and it swung shut, cutting her off from the light, but a second later it swung back open and he stepped into the hall with her, at most twenty feet away now.

Glancing back over her shoulder, Cora saw the dark square of a doorway not far off. If I can make it there, she thought, I'll close the door and hold him off as long as I can. Her already tired arms were trembling with fatigue, and her elbows kept giving out on her. He was talking again, his voice still soft, almost gentle.

"I remember cutting your family up," he said.

He was picking up his pace, trying to lull her with the sound of his voice. Maybe he didn't know how badly she was hurt, how weak she was. Maybe he thought she was dangerous. Or maybe he was just playing with her like a cat plays with a mouse before ripping it into shreds.

"Yeah," he murmured, "I killed your mother and father first, and saved you and the boy for dessert. The boy was sweet, but you . . . you got away. But I've got you now, don't I?"

He lunged at her.

Cora turned and saw that the door was just behind her and to her right.

With one final heave, she pushed through it—and fell backwards into space.

She was surprised how loud her scream sounded in her own ears.

Chapter 28

Sarah was on her hands and knees in front of the entrance to the heating duct, squinting into the darkness, when she heard the scream. It was faint and far off, but she was sure she'd heard it. Cora.

She stood up and turned to Cole, trying at the same time to reach out for Cora, for any trace of the girl. But she felt nothing. She hoped that didn't mean what she was afraid it might.

"Where does this lead?" she said.

Cole thought for a moment, then said, "It goes all over the building. There's one big duct that comes up from the boiler-room, and that breaks off into . . . I don't know, at least a dozen smaller ducts." He paused briefly, then continued. "But I don't think she'll take any of the smaller ducts."

"Why?" Sarah said.

"Because the big one, the one that goes to the furnace in the basement, goes down. She's going to be one tired little girl. You don't wake up after being unconscious for a week and a half and start training for a marathon. She's going to be stiff and weak. I'm surprised she even managed to get out of the bed . . ." Cole looked in the direction of the bed and his voice fell off.

"What is—" Sarah followed his sight line and saw what he'd fixed on. She hadn't seen it before, because she'd been so preoccupied with the rest of the mess in the room and with trying to figure out where Cora might have gone, but she sure as hell saw it now, and it scared her powerfully.

The railing on the side of the bed had been ripped to pieces. It was peeled back—no, Sarah thought, it was blown out, like a flower, away from the bed.

"Jesus," Cole said, running his hand over a segment of the mangled metal. "What the hell could have done this?"

Sarah and Cole locked eyes for a moment, and in her gaze Cole got the answer he needed. He nodded and swore again, shaking his head.

"How far from the boiler room are we?" Sarah said.

"Not far. The stairs to the basement are just at the end of the hall."

Even though Sarah could feel the physical agony Cole was experiencing emanating from his body like heat off a radiator, it was overshadowed by his concern for Cora, a concern nothing short of parental.

Something suddenly seemed to occur to Cole. "Wait," he said, "the base."

"What are you talking about?" Sarah said.

"Below us," Cole answered, his gaze falling to the floor, "there's an old submarine base. It's been closed down for years, but a few years ago we lost a patient to it, a child. There are levels and levels . . . Come on, we have to hurry." Cole started for the door.

"Wait," she said, stopping. "What about the killer?" She swept an arm around the room at the destruction Luis had caused. "He'll be after her."

"Then let's arm ourselves," Cole said. He headed for the wall near the exit and opened the door of the first aid cabinet that was mounted there. He searched around inside for a moment, then pulled out a long, thin object wrapped in white paper. He tore the wrapper off, exposing a disposable, black-handled scalpel. The blade was flimsy, but it was better than nothing.

Turning back to Sarah, he found her holding the IV tree over her head. With a grunt, she brought it down, breaking the glass over the face of the big machine on the floor. She dropped the metal tree and poked through the glass purposefully, finally pulling out a six-inch jagged shard.

Using the shard like a knife, being careful not to cut herself, she quickly sliced free a strip of the white sheet on Cora's bed, then wrapped the swatch of cloth around the butt end of the shard, forming a makeshift dagger.

"Okay," she said, testing the dagger's weight in her hand, "let's go."

The door to the stairwell leading down to the boiler-room stood slightly open.

"He's down there," Cole said. "That door has been locked for three years. It's only opened now when the furnace needs maintenance." He paused for a second, then added, "Weird. Unless this guy had a key, there's no way he should have been able to open this door, not without breaking it down or shooting it open."

"Maybe he did break it in," Sarah said.

"No," Cole replied. "Look, the door opens into the hall, not into the stairwell, so he couldn't have. Anyway, these doors are solid metal. It would take a stick of dynamite to get through one of these suckers."

"So maybe he had a stick of dynamite."

"Right," Cole whispered, "or maybe he just made bad jokes until the door couldn't stand it anymore."

A brief but searing bolt of fear and panic hit Sarah like lightning, sending her staggering backwards, away from the door. For a moment she didn't understand where it had come from. What could have frightened her so badly? And then she understood; it wasn't her fear.

"What is it?" Cole said, coming to her and taking her arm. Open and vulnerable as she was, Cole's worry and pain flooded uncontrollably into her mind.

An image sprung at her.

She saw herself buried to the neck in sand, immobile in the heavy wetness, waves of the rising tide crashing around her, over her, her mouth gaping open, hollows of her eyes filled with cold sea-water, lungs crushed by the weight of the sand and by the lack of air . . .

Sarah wanted to answer Cole, to tell him what was happening, but she couldn't, couldn't . . .

She yanked her arm out of his grasp and stumbled to the wall, bracing her back against it, leaning over, hands on her knees, trying to draw breath. Cole stood back, understanding.

Slowly, slowly, she reconstructed her wall. One brick, one breath, one brick, one breath. She blocked everything else out. There was just her and her wall. Though it only took a minute, maybe even less, to Sarah it felt like an hour.

When she could, she looked up at Cole.

"It's okay," she said. She could no longer feel the full force of the fear which had assaulted her just moments before, but the power of it was so intense that even now, with her wall up, she could feel something out there, something which wanted in.

She'd dropped her makeshift dagger on the floor, and now she picked it up.

"She's down there," Sarah said, "and we have to go get her. We have to find her before he does."

Cole in the lead, they descended the stairs.

Chapter 29

Only a moment after surfacing, Cora realized how fortunate she'd been to hit the water side-first instead of leading with her feet or head. The water was shallow, maybe three and a half feet deep, and if she'd have gone in any other way, she surely would have broken both her legs or cracked her head open on the floor. Hitting with her side, she'd only just kissed the floor with her back.

All around her, the darkness and water pressed in like a pair of black velvet pillows, sandwiching her, perfectly fit to the contours of her body. There was a complete absence of light.

Trying not to cry, trying not to let loose any of the sounds which threatened to slip from her mouth, Cora pushed herself backwards through the waist-high water, favoring her bad leg, using her good one to push off the floor.

Cora was disoriented, but she knew that she was underground, even that she was deep underground. After she'd fallen from the duct, she had realized that the room she'd fallen into was likely part of a basement, if only because that's where her furnace had been located at home. The last thing she'd expected when she pushed herself through the door as she fled from the killer was to fall again. But fallen she had. And far.

She'd felt herself suspended in the air for seconds, the darkness closing in on her like an embrace, and then the water had slapped her face and right side like a thousand stinging hands and sucked her in, filling her mouth and nose and ears with liquid ice.

Cora covered her eyes, as, with a shocking suddenness, she was bathed in light from high above.

The first feeling she registered was shock. Not at having been so quickly rediscovered, but at how far away the light came from.

Revealed in the glow of the killer's flashlight, the elevator shaft sprang into sharp relief. Between the bottom of the shaft, where she stood hip deep in water, and the killer, there were at least three floors, each marked with blocky, black numbers. She couldn't see the number of the level where the killer stood and from which she'd apparently fallen, but to her right, beside the open door which represented the only exit from the elevator shaft on this level, there was a large, black 4.

Abruptly, the flashlight swung away, and Cora saw a large, dark form step out into the shaft and start down toward her, presumably on a ladder, though Cora couldn't see it if there was one.

With no forethought, she turned toward the door she'd seen and fled, lurching forward through the water, dragging her bad leg.

Moving blindly, not knowing where she was moving to but only that it was away, Cora heard a loud splash from somewhere behind and let out a startled squeak. The killer; he'd already finished his climb down the wall of the shaft. Jesus, he was fast.

Cora stopped and let herself float, peeling her ears for any further sound, any indication that the killer knew which way she had gone and was closing on her, but there was only silence.

As quietly as possible, she pushed ahead, adrenaline and fear pumping through her veins, giving her strength she didn't have any right to.

She groped out in front of her, feeling for the wall. When she didn't feel it, she turned to her right, and in seconds her hand encountered it. All her pain momentarily forgotten, Cora slid along with her hand pressed to the concrete, breathing in ragged gasps.

There was suddenly nothing but open air beneath her hand and she turned to the right, into what she hoped was a room, not another hallway.

Just a few steps later her hip slammed into something hard and unmoving, sending shivers down her leg and through her pelvic bone.

Cora put her hands down and encountered a dry, dusty surface.

Something soft and furry and squeaking scampered over her wrist.

Cora squealed and jerked her hand away, then, realizing it was most likely only a rat, steeled herself and placed her hand back on the desk, sweeping her forearm over the dry surface. With shrieks of outraged indignation, several large bodies splashed into the water.

With a hiss of pain as her injured leg scolded her, Cora heaved herself up onto the desk and huddled with her back against the wall. Shivering from the cold, she pulled her legs into her chest with her hands and hugged them, trying to ignore the hot, angry throbbing in her knee and hip.

Think, she told herself, *don't panic. You'll die if you panic. Just calm down and think.*

Doing everything she could to block out the chill and the pain, Cora cleared her mind until it was entirely black, until she was as dark inside as it was outside. Then, reaching out with a spidery thin filament of her mind, she searched the darkness for Sarah, for the spark of light that would mean Sarah was close, but she saw nothing, felt nothing. God, where was she?

Chapter 30

So strongly had Sarah built the wall around her mind that Cora's weak probe only bounced off and died in the darkness, doing nothing more than alerting Sarah that something might briefly have been there, but wasn't anymore.

As soon as she felt it, Sarah came to a stop in the waist-high water and dropped her guard just the tiniest bit, opening herself, but it was already too late, and Cora's silent cry was gone. And unlike words spoken aloud, of this cry there was no echo.

"What is it?" Cole said, turning back to her. He was a few feet ahead, holding the black-handled scalpel up out of the water with one hand, the flashlight with the other.

"Nothing," Sarah said, "I thought I might have felt something . . . but it was nothing." The silence of Cora's thoughts worried Sarah, especially since the noise of her fear had been strong and constant until a few minutes ago, until just after they had finished the climb down the elevator shaft. It was exactly that fear which Sarah had been counting on to lead them to her, but all of the sudden the signals had ceased, leaving only a stifling silence. In the absence of a signal from Cora, they were left with little choice than to perform a room-by-room search of the entire level, hoping that Sarah's intuition was right, and that Cora was really on this floor.

Cole nodded. "It's okay. Let's keep moving. We'll find her."

They moved ahead, trying to be as quiet as possible, not an easy task since every time they took a step, they sent ripples of water sloshing up against the cinder-block walls, disturbing all of the garbage which crowded the flooded hall.

As Cole panned the flashlight back and forth across the hall, Sarah got a good look at the amount of trash littering the place.

When the Navy had deserted the base, they had apparently left much of what they no longer wanted behind, including bed frames, desks, chairs, and box upon box of what looked like books and files and office supplies. Much of this waterlogged detritus had been piled high in the hall, and even though they had walked only thirty or forty feet since leaving the elevator shaft, they had already needed to inch through several narrow gaps sideways to progress down the hall. This was nerve-wracking work, since each time they came to a new obstacle, they never knew whether there would be a knife-wielding murderer waiting for them on the other side.

"Wait a minute," Cole said. It snapped Sarah from her meditation on the garbage.

He was standing still, looking back in the direction they'd come.

"What's wrong?" Sarah said.

"Even if we do find Cora," Cole said, "how are we going to find our way out of here? It's like a maze. We could walk in circles for hours and freeze to death."

"We can worry about that once we find her."

"No," Cole said. "This place goes on forever, and you may not be too cold now, but you will be soon."

"Believe me," she answered, "I'm plenty cold now, sweetheart." She could see how eager he was to get moving again, echoing the way she felt, but he was forcing himself to think ahead. Even if they did find her, they would still have to get out of the base. He was right, she decided. They needed to figure out some way to mark their path. "Okay," she said, "so what do we do? I left my ball of yarn at home. You remember yours?"

"Fresh out," he said.

Sarah thought hard for a moment, searching for an answer. Her eyes passed over a rickety bed frame propped against the wall a short distance away. A bar hung loose from the top, one end broken and jagged. She stepped to it and, using a back and forth motion, pried the bar off. It gave way with a scream of metallic protest and came off in her hand.

"Shine that over here for a second," she said, walking to one of the walls.

Although the Navy's pride in the place seemed to have ended when they deserted it, the builders of the base had apparently cared a bit more, enough to use high-quality paint on the walls. Even now, after so many years of moisture and neglect, the white paint was glossy and unchipped.

Bracing the dull end of the length of metal against the crook of her arm, Sarah scraped the sharp end hard against the wall in a horizontal line, moving the bar rapidly back and forth. Flecks of white paint fell from the wall and into the water.

In moments, Sarah had managed to clear a foot-long strip of the paint from the wall and quickly added the two shorter lines of an arrowhead at the end facing back toward the elevator shaft. Stepping away, she said, "There."

She saw Cole smiling at her. "Not quite Hansel and Gretel," he said, "but I guess it'll do."

Sarah rested the bar on her shoulder like a musketeer carrying his gun. "All right," she said, "problem solved. Onward ho."

They moved on, easing their way around another of the jutting stacks of piled debris.

There was a door coming up on the right and they slowed down, inching forward through the water.

Cole directed the beam of the flashlight down at the water, dropping the hallway into near complete darkness. In the gloom, Sarah saw him take a tighter grip on the flimsy scalpel and raise it above his shoulder. Then he slipped through the doorway. Sarah followed him, squeezing the rag-wrapped hilt of her glass knife, feeling tight-chested and scared.

The room was empty, or unoccupied, at any rate. There were things in it, dozens of things, but no people, which was both good news and bad.

The room was fairly small, perhaps ten feet by ten feet, the walls the same white-painted cinderblock. Lining the side of the room directly opposite the doorway were a series of narrow wooden compartments, each about a foot wide. From the left side of each cubbyhole a wooden peg jutted. On some of the pegs, black things were draped.

On another of the white walls, a long metal strip had been mounted at head level. Things hung from it, too.

"What are those?" Sarah said, nodding over at the black things hanging on the pegs.

Cole waded over to one of the cubbyholes and ran his fingers over the black object hanging in it. "Neoprene," he said. "They're wetsuits." He took the suit off the hook, then moved to the next cubbyhole and grabbed another of the suits.

Sarah made her way over to the other wall and took one of the long black things in her hand, reassured by Cole's report. "Air hoses," she added. "This must have been a dive-prep room."

"Here," Cole said, then tossed Sarah one of the suits he'd

taken down, "put this on. We're losing body heat fast in this water."

In her eagerness to resume their search, Sarah almost objected, but he was right. After just a few minutes of wading through the hip-high water, she was already losing the feeling in her legs, except for a numb throbbing in her knees and ankles. She sat down on a desktop sticking up out of the water and shucked off her sweatpants, then pulled the wetsuit on. It was too big for her and bunched at the waist, but she could already feel some of the warmth returning to her legs.

"Need a zip?" Sarah turned around at the sound of Cole's voice. He had managed to get his own suit on up to the waist, and the top was hanging down into the water. There was no way he was going to get the arms on without some serious pain.

"Sure," she said.

Cole ran the zipper up the back of her suit-top.

The tickling feeling Sarah had felt before in her head returned suddenly and this time she acted fast, dropping her wall almost all the way, searching for the source.

Cora, she thought, *stay with me. Don't go away.*

Sarah, Cora's frightened voice came back to her, weak and almost imperceptible, *help me, please!*

The pain in the girl's transmission was unmistakable, and Sarah wondered if the killer had already found her and was cutting her even as they stood here talking.

The look on her face must have been strange, because she heard Cole ask her what was going on.

"It's her," Sarah said, "I have her, Cole."

Chapter 31

Luis felt the girl spring to life in his head and whirled around, half-expecting to find her standing right behind him, but other than himself and the dozen or so empty oxygen tanks piled in the corner, the small room was empty.

Closing his eyes, he moved his head back and forth, barely breathing, like a wolf testing the wind for the scent of blood, for the smell of its wounded prey.

There. There it was. Not as strong as it had been before, but he could follow it. Oh yes, he had her now.

Opening his eyes again, Luis moved back toward the door he'd come in just moments before.

This was the tenth or fifteenth room he'd searched in the last twenty minutes, and almost without realizing it, Luis had progressed quickly from a state of exalted triumph to near-paralyzing terror.

Stepping out of the elevator shaft the girl had fallen down, Luis had set off quickly after the girl, feeling her strongly in his mind, close. He'd known he would make quick work of her and be on his way in no time, his life his own once more. He'd turned down hall after hall, paying little attention to where he was going, and then, just as he felt that he was closing in on her, she had vanished, disappeared.

For the first time he had felt the darkness all around him.

Quickly, he had searched room after room, but took the time to be thorough. Even more horrible than the idea of not finding the girl at all was the possibility of passing right over her in the darkness without ever knowing it.

And now, out in the hallway again, Luis stopped and looked both ways down the short corridor. At one end, fifty or so feet from where he stood, a red fire door stood open. At the other, Luis could see a flight of stairs through the open stairwell door. The way out.

Grinning once more, he turned toward the fire door, toward the girl.

Chapter 32

Cora was startled from the trance-like state into which she'd fallen by a loud screeching sound, which was followed immediately by the thump of something heavy banging into a wall. A door opening, she thought, and close.

Through the open door of the room she was in, Cora saw the yellow beam of a flashlight flicker over the walls of the hallway just outside.

The killer; he'd found her. She never should have tried to reach out to Sarah again!

Cursing her stupidity, Cora severed her connection with Sarah and forced her mind to return to blackness, then slowly straightened out her legs, biting back a scream as the tight quadriceps and hamstring muscles in both her upper legs spasmed and threatened to cramp on her. She waited for the atrophied muscles to relax, eyes focused on the brightening light out in the hallway. The light was now accompanied by sloshing sounds as the killer grew ever closer. She could see small ripples on the surface of the water in the light.

Waiting was no longer an option; he'd be on top of her in seconds. It was act now or die.

Biting the inside of her cheek, Cora slid back into the cold water, feet first, easing herself in as quietly as possible.

The killer was right outside the room now, and the light was bright enough for Cora to be able to see her surroundings for the first time.

The room into which she'd wandered was enormous, at least fifty feet long and half as wide. The middle of the room was dominated by an oval-shaped table, the top of which was the only part visible above the water. Dozens of brown bodies scampered over the large surface of the table, zipping around in a seeming frenzy, excited by the light.

Chairs surrounded the table, but only their high backs protruded from the water, like the tops of tombstones in a flooded cemetery.

There was little else in the room, save for the small desk upon which Cora had taken shelter from the water.

No more time. He was here.

Taking a quick breath, Cora ducked beneath the water just as the bright circle of the flashlight head swung around the edge of the doorway.

She groped back behind herself with one hand, pushing up against the water with her other, trying to keep herself under. Her searching hand found and latched onto the leg of the desk and she pulled herself backwards, underneath it.

The small breath she'd managed to snatch before going under was rapidly expiring. Her once voluminous lungs were now unfit for this kind of thing. If she didn't get air soon, she was going to pass out.

As slowly as she could, Cora rose toward the surface. The top of her head thunked softly against the bottom of the desk. Begging for a break, any little break, Cora angled her head back.

Between the water and the bottom of the desktop there were maybe three inches of space. Cora pressed her face into the narrow sliver of air and sucked hungrily at the oxygen, trying not to splash.

Out in the room, the light was moving off toward the big table. If she could only keep quiet for a couple more minutes, she just might make it out of this. Breathing in shallow gasps, Cora concentrated on the blackness in her mind. *Black black black.*

Sharp claws were suddenly digging into the skin of her cheeks. Unable to stop herself, Cora jerked up, banging her head on the desk, and swiped at the rat with both hands, knocking it back into the water with a splash. She heard it swim off.

Shaking, she peered out from underneath the table.

The light had stopped and was moving back toward her.

Oh, fuck, Cora thought. *Please, please let him think it was just a rat, please . . .*

She held her breath, trying to think of what she would do if he reached under the table. *Bite,* she thought, *bite and scratch and kick. Anything to live. Anything.*

The light stopped no more than ten feet from where she hid and swept over the water and the desk. Cora saw the yellow circle of light illuminate a swimming rat less than five feet from her. There was a dot of red on the fur between its bulging eyes, and she wondered if it was her own blood.

Suddenly, there was a painful twinge from her left hamstring and she felt it beginning to bunch. No, she begged, not now, not now . . .

The light moved away from the desk and headed back in the direction of the big table.

Unable to wait any longer, Cora maneuvered her legs out from underneath her, stretching them out beneath the water in front of her.

But the hamstring cramped anyway.

She threw her head back in pain, the tendons in her neck standing out like stands of thin rope. The pain was so intense that she couldn't have screamed even if she'd wanted to. A hiss of air was all that escaped from her constricted throat.

Frantically, she reached down and massaged the cramped muscle with both hands. The hamstring was a hard ball underneath her fingers, like a fist in her leg. She worked it like a ball of dough, kneading it ferociously. Finally, it began to loosen up and she could breathe again.

Shaking, she ventured a peek out and saw that the killer had stopped again near the huge table. He spoke.

"Is she in here?"

Another voice, this one a woman's, familiar. "I don't know. I thought so, but she's gone again now. I lost her again."

Sarah! Cora pushed herself out from underneath the desk, the horrible pain of just moments before forgotten.

"Over here!" she yelled, but her voice was rusty from lack of use and her words came out barely a whisper. She slapped the water with both hands and was instantly bathed in light.

Sarah reached her in moments and pulled her into a powerful hug.

"I knew you'd find me," Cora whispered into Sarah's ear, arms wrapped around her neck.

"Damn straight, sweetie," Sarah whispered back fiercely, "but we're not out of this yet."

Chapter 33

With Sarah and Cole supporting Cora between them, one of her arms slung around each of their shoulders, the three of them followed the arrows Sarah had been making at every turn back in the direction of the elevator shaft.

Although they did their best to keep the pace brisk, Sarah was finding it more and more difficult to deny the pain and stiffness sinking into the joints of her legs. The water had felt merely cold at first, then after a while she had ceased to feel it at all, but now the cold was back and more intense than ever. With every step she took, it felt like pieces of broken glass were grating in the joints of her knees and hips.

"How much farther do you think it is?" Cole said, gasping for breath. Though he had been a rock throughout this ordeal and was still going strong, Sarah could tell that Cole was really beginning to tire. She could sympathize; though Cora was light and did what she could to help them along, bearing half of the girl's weight in addition to her own was rapidly draining Sarah's strength.

"I don't know," she answered, "I lost track. Just keep following the arrows. We'll get there."

Cora said something, but it was too quiet to hear over the splashing sounds of their bodies moving through the water.

"What?" Sarah said, plunging ahead, eyes searching the darkness ahead for any sign of movement.

The girl spoke again, this time louder, more firmly. "I said, stop."

"Why?" Sarah asked, "What's wrong?" Hearing Cora's words, Cole had also stopped and turned the light toward the two women, bathing them in light.

"What's going on?" he said. "I think we're getting close. The shaft's just up ahead."

Cora shook her head. "No," she said, "he's up there, waiting."

"How do you know that?" Cole said.

"I can feel him," Cora said, "close."

"Are you sure?" Sarah said.

Cora nodded. "He's there, waiting for us."

Cole was about to say something more when there was suddenly a bright flash from somewhere down the hall in the direction they'd been walking. A split second later, the report of the gun reached them, a deafening WHACK!

As Sarah watched, Cole's shirt ruffled, as if in a light breeze, and his free hand moved slowly to his side, where a small flower of blood was appearing, just above his hip. His mouth and eyes were open wide in an expression of utmost surprise.

There was another flash and a WHACK, like someone banging an iron griddle against a stone wall, and Sarah felt the bullet whiz past her cheek. For a very brief moment, she felt totally incapable of movement. She was marble, a statue. Paralyzed.

And then Cole's arm was around her and pushing her through the door on her right. He'd released Cora and was trying to shepherd them out of the killer's line of fire, his left hand still clamped to his side.

Sarah stumbled under Cora's weight, bearing it now all by herself, but managed to remain upright.

"Move!" Cole yelled, plunging through the door behind her. "Don't stop." He pointed the flashlight at a door on the opposite side of the room they had just entered. "Keep moving, Sarah. Go!"

They took a quick succession of turns without the slightest clue of where they were going, just trying to distance themselves from the killer. Though just moments before, Cora's weight had seemed almost unmanageable, Sarah now bore it easily. She thought that if she needed to, she could have hiked Everest with the girl strapped to her back. Blood rushed in her ears, and Sarah realized as she followed the beam of the flashlight through door after door that the abnormal surge of strength was from adrenaline. She just hoped it would hold up for a little longer. Whenever the rush ended, she would be dead in the water.

"Hold on a second," Cole said softly, coming to a halt. He leaned up against the wall, groaning in pain. He caught Sarah's eyes and smiled wanly, then lifted up the left side of his shirt and examined the wound the bullet had left, shining the light down on it.

It was lower down on his side than Sarah had first thought, near his hipbone. There was some blood seeping from it, but not too much. As gunshot wounds went, Sarah thought, Cole had come away pretty lucky. He seemed to think the same.

"Could be worse," Cole muttered. He stripped off the sweatshirt he was wearing and, holding it by the sleeves, flipped it over a couple of times. That done, he wrapped the sleeves around his waist, positioning the thickest part of the bundle over the wound. Wincing, he pressed the makeshift bandage against the bullet hole.

"Are you okay?" Sarah asked. She looked back over her shoulder, fully expecting to feel a bullet plow into her back at any second. She wondered whether she would hear the report or feel the bullet first. Absurdly, it occurred to her to ask Cole for his thoughts on the subject. She quelled the urge.

"For the time being," Cole replied, and Sarah loved him intensely in that moment for his courage. "How did he find us so easily?" Cole asked. "If this place is as big as it seems, there's no way he should have been able to find us so quickly. It's like he knew right where we were."

"It's me," Cora said. "He can feel my thoughts. I was trying to find Sarah, but he must have felt it, too."

"Can you hide yourself? Lock your mind or something, so he can't feel you?"

Cora nodded. "I think so."

"Good," Cole said. He hesitated a moment, then said, "Can you feel him now?"

"Yes," Cora said. "He's close, but not too close. We have a little time."

"Good," Cole said again.

"Cole," Sarah said, "we should keep moving while we're ahead of him. We're giving him time to catch up to us."

Cole shook his head. "We can't just keep running, Sarah. I can't carry her much longer with my arm like this, and I don't think you can do it alone. Can you?"

Sarah wanted badly to say yes, but she forced herself to be honest. "No, I can't, but if we can just find the shaft, or the stairs—"

"Even if we did," Cole broke in, "even if we managed to get out of here and back up to the Clinic, we'd have no way off the island, and sooner or later he'd figure out what was going on and he'd come looking for her up there."

"What are you saying?" Sarah asked. "That you want to confront this psycho? That's nuts!"

"No," Cora said softly, "he's right."

"What?" Sarah turned and looked at her incredulously.

221

"He's not going to stop until I'm dead," Cora said. "Wherever I run, wherever we run, he'll find us. I know he will. I can feel it."

For a long moment, Sarah was silent. Finally, she looked at Cole and said, "Okay, I guess you might be right."

"Wow," Cole said, smiling, knowing how scared Sarah was and what kind of discipline it was taking for her to stay calm, "that's something I never heard you say during the three years we were together."

She bunched up her hand into a loose fist and punched him lightly in his good arm. "Very funny, asshole."

Cole grabbed her hand and squeezed it tightly for a moment, then said, "I've got an idea. I saw something a couple rooms back we might be able to use, but I have to ask you something, Cora." He turned to the girl, and she returned his stare evenly.

"You want to know if I was the one who broke the bed in my room upstairs," Cora said.

Cole nodded. "And I want to know if you can do something like that again when you need to."

Chapter 34

She'd been in his sights, and still, she'd escaped. And now, like before, she'd vanished from his mind again! What was it going to take to kill this little cunt?

Luis slashed out with the razor at a fluorescent bulb hanging down from the ceiling by a wire and the long tube dropped into the water with a splash, the wire cleanly severed. The tube floated on the surface for a moment, like a long, white maggot, then slowly sank.

He'd been surprised twenty minutes earlier when he turned the corner and saw the three of them making their way towards him down the hall. He had no idea who the man and the woman were, but instead of feeling alarm, he saw them only as impediments to the achievement of his goal, slicing the whore-child into meat confetti.

Though he hadn't wanted to use the gun to kill the girl, it had seemed perfectly acceptable to use it to get rid of the others. He'd gotten off only two quick shots before they disappeared through a door just to their right, but he was pretty sure he'd clipped one of them. As he passed by the place they had first come into sight, he'd been glad to see the spatter of blood on the wall near the door, and a bloody handprint on the doorjamb a couple of rooms later.

Luis walked now with the razor and flashlight in one hand, and the Glock in the other. Every room he passed through, he followed standard police procedure. Check left, right, each corner, the ceiling, behind the door, any nooks and crannies where someone might be able to fit, then move on to the next room and do it all over again.

But now he was getting cold. Really cold.

Born and raised in the northern part of Washington State, Luis was used to being exposed to extreme conditions for long periods of time, but wading for almost an hour through water which was a couple degrees above freezing was pushing it. The joints of his legs were trying to freeze up on him, and his body was shaking enough that he could hear the batteries clacking around inside the tube of the flashlight.

Taking a deep breath, Luis stepped into the next room and performed a quick search, then moved on.

What if they've gone back up top? The thought stopped him. *What if they found a way to the surface and are calling for help even now?* But the thought froze him for only a moment. Even if they had managed to find a way back up, and he doubted very much that they could have discovered one so quickly, it would take hours for help to arrive, and by then all that would be left to do was slide the corpses into body bags. He had time. No sweat.

The scream pierced his mind like a rusty needle.

Luis dropped the Glock and only just managed to keep hold of the flashlight and razor.

Reeling in pain, he clapped his wrists to his ears, trying to block out the shrill scream, but it didn't work. The scream continued, its volume undiminished, and Luis was just able to understand through the pain that the scream wasn't in the air around him, but in his mind.

And then it was gone.

Luis stood still, hands still pressed against the sides of his head, waiting for it to return. Warmth trickled down his cheeks and from his nose, and Luis tasted the coppery tang of blood on his lips.

Slowly, he dropped his hands and straightened up.

Though the hall ahead was dark, Luis found that he was able to see. A white luminescence, like smoke, filled the air.

"What?" Luis said under his breath. He wondered if the scream he'd felt in his head had somehow affected his vision, torn something in his brain. Maybe this was some kind of hallucination, a signal of the beginning of the end.

Without knowing quite why, he found the on/off button of the flashlight and pushed it. The beam blinked off.

All around him, the shapes of things were visible. He could see! But that was impossible. There were no windows; there couldn't be. He was at least fifty feet below the surface of the island.

Luis looked around for another light source, but found nothing. There was only the white smoke, hanging there at eye level, unmoving.

It hung in the air like a solid thing, like thickly wadded white sheets, twisted together. Luis raised a shaking hand to touch it, but his fingers only passed through, trailing little wisps of white vapor that he could not feel. He raised his fingers to his nose to sniff, but there was no odor.

Stepping back away from the smoke, Luis followed it with his eyes to where it vanished through a doorway some fifty feet from where he stood.

And Luis began to understand. The smoke was no different from the signal that had drawn him all the way across the country from L.A. It was just a more powerful version, amplified to the umpteenth power until it was no longer simply an indefinable urge, but an actual, visible trail.

And it would lead him right to her.

Slipping the flashlight butt-first into the waistband of

his pants near the small of his back, Luis moved forward, following the smoke, now gripping only the razor in his hand.

The smoke twisted through the door and across the large room it led to, then out the other side of the room where Luis could see it took an abrupt right turn.

"Stupid bitch," he muttered, smiling, energized, and moving fast.

He followed the trail down a long hallway and up to a heavy metal portal. The door was red, like the one he'd passed through earlier, and it was shut almost completely. The trail of white snaked through, but the opening wasn't large enough to admit a man.

Luis pulled at the edge of the door, but the hinges must have been rusty, because it didn't budge an inch. He placed the open razor between his teeth and took a grip on the edge of the door with both hands.

Propping his left foot against the wall, he pulled as hard as he could. After a moment when he was sure the door wouldn't move at all, it jerked open about half a foot, just enough to allow him entrance to the chamber beyond.

On the other side of the door was a small room, only a few feet wide, and then another of the thick doors. Each of the doors had a wheel mounted on it, presumably to spin it locked. Beyond the little chamber, there was a huge one.

This appeared to be where the submarines had docked. The space of the chamber was dominated by an enormous, round pool, at least fifty yards wide, the lip of which stood about five feet higher than the level of the water, which was undisturbed. Whatever equipment the room had once housed had been cleared out long ago, and only wires and pulleys remained, hanging from the high ceiling.

There were two doors in and out of the chamber: the one

Luis had just entered through, and one on the other side of the room. The trail of white smoke led there.

It was only when he was just a few feet from the door that he saw the girl.

As with the door on the other side of the large chamber, this one consisted of two heavy red doors and the airlock in-between.

The girl was slumped down in the water on the other side of the airlock, leaning against the wall, only her head and shoulders visible above the water. Her eyes were closed, head tilted to the side so her cheek lay against her shoulder. Luis couldn't tell if she was breathing. The ribbon of white vapor tapered off just feet from her.

Stepping closer, he saw that the girl's chest was moving very slowly. And he could also see now that each breath carried with it a little puff of white that drifted over to join the swath Luis had followed.

He stepped into the airlock, holding the razor out away from his body, ready to slash. He was aware of how ideal a spot this was for an ambush, but there was no way in hell the girl, or the man and woman with her, were going to budge the airlock doors, not when even he could barely move one half a foot. He moved toward the motionless girl.

Luis registered the movement behind him just a split second too late, and with a resounding BOOM the door swung shut behind him, hinges shrieking protest. He turned and pushed at the door, but heard the wheel spinning on the other side as the bolts slid home.

Turning back around to look for the girl, he just saw her white feet as they were pulled clear of the opposite door, and then it was swinging shut, too, closing tightly, the bolts sliding home as the wheel was spun on the other side.

Luis flung himself against the door, dropping the razor

into the water, pounding the metal with his fists.

"No!" he screamed. "Open this fucking door! Let me out of here!"

Feeling black panic surging in his chest, Luis turned away from the door just as the last of the white smoke faded into darkness.

He pressed his ear up against the door, listened for voices.

"Hey!" Luis pounded hard against the metal with his fist. "Hey! You can't just leave me here! Open this fucking door! Open this door!"

Chapter 35

Standing outside the main entrance to the Davies Clinic, Steve Crothers was one unhappy cop. He'd come all this way to put an end to Argento, and now it appeared that he wasn't going to get his chance. The psychotic bastard was nowhere to be found.

Crothers took a pack of cigarettes from his coat pocket and bumped one out. He lit it and dragged deep, then blew smoke with a sigh.

When he'd arrived in Stone Beach, he'd gone directly to the police station, and from there, he'd been taken to where Argento's Mustang was found.

The snow had really been coming down by the time he and the patrolman he was sent with arrived, and any tracks Argento might have left were long since gone.

Crothers knew he was close, but he had nothing to go on. Argento could have gone anywhere from the old graveyard. It was even possible that Argento had come all this way to throw the authorities off his trail, and was even now heading back west to more familiar ground. But Crothers didn't think so.

It turned out he was right. Just minutes after returning from his survey of the old graveyard, the sheriff received a report that a small outboard boat had been stolen from the same people who, the day before, had reported their dog killed in the backyard of their house. They hadn't noticed the boat until today, because it hadn't occurred to them to check.

As soon as he hung up the phone, the sheriff, a thick man

named Jim Orange, pulled his heavy coat on and said to Crothers, "You'd better bundle up for this. Borrow a coat, if you need to."

Twenty minutes later Orange, Crothers, and a deputy were chugging out into the bay in the Stone Beach PD's thirty-foot launch, Orange at the wheel.

Luckily, the weather had been good, and it didn't take long to spot the stolen boat. It was pulled up on a clear stretch of beach, and no effort had been taken to conceal it. But their luck ended there.

After searching the island over two hours, there was still no trace of Argento, or anyone else, for that matter. If Argento had been on the island at one time, it didn't seem that he was anymore. Even the sheriff seemed doubtful. The ferry came twice a day, he said, and it would have been easy enough for him to gain passage back to the mainland that way.

Crothers finished his cigarette and went inside, rubbing his cold hands together. He was on his way back to the Clinic's office, where Orange and the deputy were on the phone to the mainland, when he saw three slumped figures emerge from the door leading downstairs to the basement. The two people on the outside were supporting the person in the middle, who looked like a child, a young girl.

One of the people in the group saw him and raised a hand and spoke. "Help." A woman's voice.

Sprinting, Crothers reached them in seconds. "I'm a police officer," he said, "it's okay now." He called loudly for Orange to come, then said, "Where's Argento?"

"Is that his name?" The man spoke softly, as though speaking any other way would be too painful. He was holding a blood-soaked clump of fabric to his side and seemed pretty banged-up in general. They all did. And soaking wet, too.

"Yeah."

"He's down there still," the woman said, her teeth clacking together from the cold.

"Is he alive?"

She nodded. "Yes. But he probably wishes he wasn't." She quickly filled him in on the details of Argento's situation. By the time she was done, Crothers knew he was smiling. Maybe he'd get his chance after all.

When Orange and his deputy arrived, Crothers went to the duty office to get blankets, then returned and wrapped several around each of them. There was a first-aid kit in the office, too, and Crothers patched the man up as well as he could. The bullet wound was serious, but not life-threatening. He would be okay.

When Crothers finished with his field dressing, Orange said, "We should get you all down to the boat before you stiffen up too bad. Let's go."

Each of the police officers helped one of the three survivors, more dragging and carrying them than helping them to walk. The process of stiffening up had long since begun, despite Orange's optimistic outlook.

"What about your boy?" Orange said to Crothers when they were back on the boat.

Crothers looked at Sarah, who was seated with her back against the transom. Though he didn't believe in such things, it felt for all the world as though she knew what he was thinking. As if to affirm this feeling, she smiled and nodded at him, as though responding to a question he'd asked. It was all the reassurance Crothers needed. He turned to Orange and said, "He's dead, Sheriff."

"That right?"

Crothers nodded.

"Well, I guess that's that, then. Throw off that line, would ya?"

Chapter 36

Sarah lay beside Cole and watched him sleep. It had been five days since the three of them had emerged from their own private hell, and normal, everyday life had never felt so sweet.

Cora had spent two nights in a hospital in Portland, mostly to make sure there were no lasting effects from the coma. As it turned out, she would be absolutely fine, and for that, Sarah was glad. For the time being, the girl was staying in a hotel near the hospital, waiting for her grandfather to be released, which should be any day now. He was recovering from the pneumonia, and just needed to regain some of his strength before going home.

Cole had also spent a night in the hospital. He'd had his wounds cleaned and sewn up, and had to wear a sling for a while, but other than his physical ailments, he seemed fine. Very fine. Surprisingly so, even.

Something had changed in him. Maybe it was that something was there which hadn't been before. Or maybe it was that something which had been inside him for so long was gone. Whatever it was, he was a changed man, a new man.

The sadness Sarah had always been able to sense coming off of him was different. It was still there, but now it was beneath in a way it hadn't been before. It no longer defined him. Maybe helping Cora had somehow absolved him, in his own mind, of some of the guilt he'd been carrying around for so long. One child had died but thanks in part to him, one had also lived. Sarah hoped he was moving along in the process of forgiving himself; God only knew he deserved to be forgiven.

She raised a hand and ran her fingers down his cheek.

"Cole," she said. He didn't answer her, but she knew he was listening. "I love you. I always have."

It took a while for him to respond, but that was okay. She knew he would eventually. "I know," he said. He opened his eyes, and they were clear and honest. They were eyes Sarah could trust. "I love you, Sarah."

And when they were done making love and were falling asleep intertwined with each other, Sarah still didn't know many things about the man she loved, but that was all right. They had time.

About the Author

Mark P. Dunn is from Swarthmore, Pennsylvania, but has lived for most of his adult life in Ohio, Maine, and North Carolina. He reads, writes, teaches, and drinks coffee, and never met a horror movie he didn't like. He can be reached at mark.dunn.1997@owu.edu.